heart failure

The Iowa School
of Letters
Award for
Short Fiction

Prize money for the
award
is provided
by a grant
from the
Iowa Arts
Council

heart failure

IVY GOODMAN

University of
Iowa Press
Iowa City

The previously published stories in this collection appear by permission:

"White Boy," *Prize Stories 1982: The O. Henry Awards.* Ed. William
Abrahams. New York: Doubleday, 1982. Originally in
Ploughshares 6, no. 4 (1981).
"Baby," *Prize Stories 1981: The O. Henry Awards.* Ed. William Abrahams.
New York: Doubleday, 1981. Originally in *Ploughshares* 5, no. 4
(1980).
"Fall Semester," "Pinecone," "Trade," "Telephones," "Resignation," "Heart
Failure," "Last Minutes," and "Revenge," *The Ark River Review:
Three Writer Issue,* 5, no. 2 (1981).
"Socialization," *The Ark River Review,* 4, no. 4 (1980).
"Documentary," *Minnesota Review,* 13 (1979).
"Telephones," *Sun & Moon,* 6/7 (1978/79).
"Fall Semester," *kayak,* 51 (1979).
"Trade," *Quarry West,* 10 (1979).
"Remnants: A Family Pattern," *Fiction,* 6, no. 1 (1979).
"Last Minutes," *Seems,* 10 (1978).

Library of Congress Cataloging in Publication Data

Goodman, Ivy, 1953 –
  Heart failure.

  (The Iowa School of Letters award for short fiction)
  Contents: Baby — Remnants — Rumpus — Bankroll —
[etc.]
  I. Title.   II. Series.
PS3557.05836H4   1983   813'.54   83 – 9183
ISBN 0 – 87745 – 119 – 2
ISBN 0 – 87745 – 120 – 6 (pbk.)

University of Iowa Press, Iowa City 52242

For Bob

CONTENTS

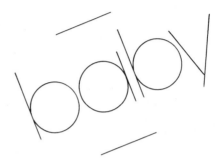

baby

H e shuttles from me, in Boston, to ex-wife and baby in Baltimore, to me, to baby. He vacations three weeks alone with baby. He wants to get to know baby. He wants custody of baby. And when he gets custody (last month he shattered a tea cup to prove how certain he is of getting custody), he wants me to help love baby. I kissed his hands, one finger bloodied, sliced by a jagged piece of china, and agreed to love baby. Already, more carefully than if they were my own, I love both the man and his baby.

Five months ago, I met the man at a party. Clearly, he wanted someone at that party. He is particular to a certain point, and then beyond that point he is not at all particular. For hours I watched him dance with a married woman who I knew would eventually refuse him. Eye to eye, hip to hip. Overheated, she took her vest off and stared at him as if that vest and the tight blue blouse beneath it mattered. Perhaps they did matter. But when she and her husband left, he came to me and talked about his baby.

"And how old is this baby?" I asked.
"Ten months."
"Do you have a photograph?"
"Not with me."
"Not in your wallet?"
"I don't have a wallet. But I have hundreds of pictures at home. Do you want to see them?"
"Yes."
"Should we go now?"
"Yes."

At least he had the integrity to wait until afterwards to bring out the baby. Naked, we sat in bed, turning over the baby in Maryland, the baby in Massachusetts, the drooling, farting, five-toothed baby, holding his toes in zoos and botanical gardens, lounging in trees, hammocks, the arms of his father, his mother. No, I was not spared the eleven duo shots of the girlish ex-wife and mother kissing the baby.

The beautiful mother of the baby. Will he go back to her? He doesn't go back. He goes on. Unknowingly, I, too, may be diminishing, a piece of the past that grows more evil with each new woman, each new recounting. The only unscathed one is that poor baby.

The baby. How does a woman who loves the father of the baby love the baby? By remembering that she is not the mother of the baby. When the father moves away, he will also take the baby. If I haven't already, I am doomed to lose both father and baby.

But why do I want them to begin with? When I could have an honest man and my own baby? Most days I am terrified by the thought of my own baby. About honest men: you must be honest in return, for who knows how long. But with the treacherous, you can be kind and honest while it lasts, knowing it won't last. In the end you suffer, of course. The surprise is how, and in which places.

Sometimes he held me all night. Sometimes when he heard me cry in sleep, he clawed my spine until I cried myself awake. When he planned a trip, I found the tickets on the bureau days before he told me he was leaving. ("By the way, I'll be flying to Maryland tomorrow." And after a pause, "Drive me to the airport at eight, would you?" Or, "Pack. You're coming with me.") For two weeks, he telephoned every midnight, though now I haven't heard his voice in sixteen days, and I tore open his last letter Saturday. It was all about the baby. The baby is walking perfectly. The baby is making friends with other babies. In so many gestures and baby words, the baby has stated his preference for road life with father, his dread of that split-level crowded with mother, grandmother, grandfather, and every baby toy available in greater Baltimore.

Yesterday, in stores, on the street, I laughed, waved, and clicked my tongue at twelve babies, wheeled, cradled, backpacked, or carefully led by twelve women; yes, all twelve, women. He is probably the only man on the Eastern Seaboard walking into a grocery at 10 A.M. without a wedding ring and with a baby. The woman he leers at over piled grapefruit will want to laugh but won't, because she's flattered, then will, because she's flattered. No wonder the baby is making friends with other babies.

But I can't compete with strangers, pretending to be lured, as I pretended to be, by his obvious glances, by his baby. He will stay with one of them or another of them, or he won't stay. He will come back, or he won't come back. Whatever his decisions, I knew from the start they would have nothing to do with me.

All last night I drifted, nearing sleep but never finding it. I miss him. According to plan, my ache spreads. I pit myself against myself. I'm losing.

I want another of our silent breakfasts, his head lowered to his bowl, his spoon overturned near his coffee mug. I want to break his mug. I want to do something to him.

He brooded. He thought he was entitled to brood. But his horrors, described on cold nights, were no more horrible than mine; he just thought they were. The stories he told and I listened to, I would never presume to tell. And if I did, who would listen to me?

Because he only liked my hair down, when I pinned it up to wash my face, I closed the bathroom door, but I closed the door for both of us. What he didn't want to see, and more, I wanted never to show him. And what he has seen I want now, impossibly, to take from him, before he mocks it to amuse his next woman.

His woman. His women. He's stuffed a battered envelope with snapshots of us, already including one of me, full lengths, with legs crossed or, in a blur, crossing, heads turning, mouths speaking. He interrupted us and then, camera swinging from his shoulder, moved on. His ex-wife, mother of the baby, is actually his third ex-wife. From the glossy pile I try to guess the first two, but can't. Bodies, faces, wives, lovers, blend. We look tired; we are tired. Thinking practically, we want a good night's sleep and wonder if he'll leave soon. But we also think our shadowed faces have been brushed by moth wings. We feel more haunted than he. When he whispered what he thought was sad, we spared him what we knew was sadder. We let him pout, in a corner, alone. But even children keep their secrets. Right now, what is he thinking? All those silent times, what was he thinking?

In a friend's house, in a crowded room, I remember looking at him. He looked back. He shook his head. He could have been bedazzled. He could have meant we'll leave soon, but not yet. Or he could have wanted me to vanish.

Is he enigmatic, or is he just myopic? He's said himself that his eyes stare when he strains them. He should wear his glasses. I wonder, alone with the baby, does he wear his glasses? As a novelty, he was married the last time in thin gold-framed glasses.

Wed in March, parents in August, estranged in November, and now, divorced, he and his ex-wife hate each other. If I said, "I'll give you another baby," would he marry me?

I don't want a baby. No, I do want a baby. I covet babies. But which are instincts, and which are yearnings? Do I feel heartbreak or the rattle of dwindling ova? What do I want so, when I lie awake, wanting? And what if I did have his baby? He would leave me and try to take the baby.

In green motel rooms, does he rest his elbows on the rails of portable cribs and watch the sleeping baby? When he slept with me, I watched him. His ribs, wings, spread, closed in, spread, closed in. He strained. I wanted to make breath easier for him.

He was losing hair. He was losing weight. His skeleton was rising out of him. Each night, new bones surprised me. My fingers stumbled. I want him again. I still want him. But my desire is diverted toward bedrolls, pillows, small animals seen from a distance, and other women's babies. Or is my desire itself diversion?

I worry about what I'll do because I know what I've done. Also, I worry about that baby.

And at dusk, when the telephone rings and I answer it, I recognize his whimper, wavering behind his father's voice, his father, who, after weeks of silence, has called to ask if I know it's raining. "Yes, here it's been raining. Where are you, where it's raining?"

"We're both in a phone booth, about ten miles south at a Texaco."

"And you're coming back?"

"Yes. Soon."

Almost before I hear them or see them, I smell them, tobacco, baby powder, wet wool, cold; and after he puts the sleeping baby on the couch and touches me, just tobacco, wool, cold. "How's the baby?"

"A pain in the neck the last hundred miles, but fine now."

The baby, his face creased by his bent cap brim, stretches one fist, then brings it close, licks it.

"His cap."

"Would you take it off? I have to get another suitcase from the car."

When I bend down, the baby turns his head; his back curls. The cap slips, and I pull it free and put it on a chair. It is that simple. In the middle of the floor, where he'll be safer, I smooth a blanket for him. When I lift him, soft, willing, but weighted down by heavy shoes, he nestles. I untie the shoes. By the time the door slams, he is covered with his own yellow quilt and still sleeping. All the while, sleeping. His father says, "You've tucked him in, thanks. Too tired to talk. Tomorrow. And nothing's settled."

No, nothing's settled. In our bedroom now, flung across the bed, the other traveler also sleeps, his trousers damp, dragged black at the cuffs from the rain. I grab his sneakers by their heels and tug. When they hit the floor, he groans, rolls. His shirt wrinkles up above his rib cage.

"Too tired to talk. Tomorrow." If he hadn't been so tired, he might have laughed at his own joke. Why now, at the end, should we talk?

In the kitchen, I sit, the only one awake in this sleeping household. I don't want the man. I don't want the baby. But when the baby cries, I go to the baby.

ased on the disorderly instructions of
Lake Greenberg, named after her
grandmother, Laka Brint Shromm,
who died the Friday before the Monday Lake was born.
Front pockets: Cut two hand-sized squares and set aside.

The twins, Drancha and Deeta Shromm, were born
to Yaakov Harold and Laka Brint Shromm during the early winter
of the couple's third married year. Drancha, who decided which
identical outfits the two would wear each day for their first nineteen
years; Drancha, who became a nurse; Drancha, who missed

second grade due to a severe back problem which left her
bedridden for seven months; Deeta, who passed second grade
alone but repeated it to keep Drancha company when she returned
to school; Deeta, who married a weak-hearted man; Deeta,
a sobbing arthritic who said she would just die without telephones,
who just died.

Legs: Double cloth and cut two. Stitch inner leg seams separately,
then baste at center front, crotch, and center back. Join
permanently, easing fullness and matching notches.

Laka Brint, born on the new continent and
accustomed to jewelry from her father's shop and black silk stockings
embroidered with white sheaves of wheat, shaved her head during
the sweat of a scarlet fever. The only hair that grew back was
a very soft down.

With seven brothers, Yaakov Harold Sh_____,
a journeyman tailor, fled his homeland to escape conscription and
marauding bands of Cossacks. On the new continent officials
certified some of the eight youths Shromms, some Shramms, though
they were all brothers from the same region, all sharing the same
harsh name together. Yaakov was a Shromm and with his savings
bought a fringed horse and matching fringed wagon and peddled
housewares through the provinces. When he stopped at the town
of P_____ and sold Mrs. Brint a metal colander and spools of
gray and red thread at her open kitchen door, he met Laka, who
was bald but beautiful. They were married that fall.

As a wedding present, Mr. Brint gave the couple
a hillside men's clothing and tailoring shop with a two-story
apartment above the store. Its kitchen led onto a dank yard and
a cobblestone alleyway.

"Personally, I'm surprised that anyone married
her," Brint said to his brother over poached fish at the luncheon
after the ceremony.

"Don't complain," his brother said.

"Did I? Oh, no. I'm thankful."

After they returned from a weekend trip to a

seashore resort, Laka cooked all morning, every morning, and at noontime set the table for a hot meal on Yaakov's treadle sewing machine. She crocheted seashells found on her honeymoon onto the borders of doilies and napkins. She organized flatware. She planted moss in iron pots around the yard walls. At night when she slid off Yaakov's thimbles, he whispered to her and stroked her tufts of hair.

Zigzag topstitching sprawling the entire finished garment: Zigzag, everywhere.

Laka conceived during the fourth month of her marriage, and from the tenth week of pregnancy on, was incapacitated. Her separating pelvic bones painfully pinched her sciatic nerve, her breasts tingled, she was constipated, and both ankles and seven toes swelled. She lay on the floral chaise lounge in the second parlor, silver needles, crochet hooks, skeins of pastel baby yarn, three yards of ribbon trim, and white linen infant smocks, merely basted together and waiting to be sewn, scattered around her. Her mother, upright on a straight-backed arm chair, started a new row of her knitting and said, "Be stern with yourself, Laka. Sit up. Start stitching."

Laka moaned and readjusted a towel over her head. "Oh, close the drapes, Mother. The light bothers me. What did you just say? I didn't hear you."

The baby kicked often and terrified Laka when she felt the shape of its foot bulging out of her stomach. "Yaakov," she whispered in the middle of the night, catching her breath again, letting go of the brass rung of their headboard. "What is it growing inside me?"

The delivery was speedy but left the imprint of forceps on the baby's head. Named Dovid, he refused his mother's aching breasts and alone in his crib, trembled. He didn't sit until he was two, he didn't walk until he was three, and when he talked at four, his words vibrated with his shudders.

Detail, front pockets: Hem all edges. Add zigzags.

With Dovid creeping about between her legs, Laka swelled with two more babies. Four feet kicked at her, and she doubled over. She napped and dreamed her stomach was glass and saw an eight-limbed creature growing bristles and claws within her. "A monster," she told her mother. To Yaakov she said, "I hope for something better," and handed him Dovid.

"I blame the doctor," Yaakov said to everyone, to strangers whose clothes he tailored. While Laka rested, Dovid twitched in the store among pants legs and knocked over boxes.

"Twins?" Laka asked after laboring. A nurse handed her scowling Drancha and the tinier Deeta. "Twins?"

"It's compensation," Yaakov told her.

When the cranky twins learned to walk, Dovid learned with them. He stumbled through the house shaking dead fowls in his hands, trailing feathers, laughing while the twins ran to hide in their closet. They were frightened of trees; he waved branches in their faces and made them look up at elms. "Red birds," he would say, pointing skyward. They would glance up, expecting cardinals, and shriek when they saw only treetops.

His mother swatted him with brooms and said, "This hurts me more than you, Dovid," while in a garbled voice he shouted out, "Police! Help! She's beating a cripple."

Fob pocket: Cut a one-inch slit at rib level and bind with strips of folded cloth (see diagram). Then stitch shut because the watch is lost.

Ephraim was Laka's and Yaakov's fourth-born, a pale, bruise-kneed child who walked the town holding his left forefinger in his right hand. At three, he was the first in the family to wear eyeglasses. For close work, such as copying in his blue copybooks, he also peered through a small magnifying lens. While the twins uprooted moss in the yard and Dovid cursed them from the kitchen steps, Ephraim lay on his stomach in the alleyway behind them, reading newspapers and selected copybooks. He was run over and killed there by a man driving a convertible.

Back pocket: Cut crookedly then stitch on left rear without bobbin thread. When the pocket falls off, reattach quickly with a straight pin.

Marvya was the baby Shromm, the last-born, the reckless one who stuffed tailored trousers meant for delivery down sewer grates, tore her coat on fences, owned a bicycle, was a Yo-Yo champ until she died, and during high school, played basketball. She never married. "But I won't die a virgin," she told her mother on the morning of her nineteenth birthday. For five years, until a friend explained it, she believed the stain of her menses was the blood of dying babies. "What luck, another miscarriage," she shouted monthly from her bedroom.

Over vest: Use a thick, opaque fabric, but to no avail because the back and fronts are too short, and there aren't any fasteners.

They were a wonderful family, standing arm in arm by the kitchen wall in their photographs. But one was killed, one went crazy, two were exactly alike, not much even when added together, and the last was defective to begin with. The wigged mother died a slow death of diabetes, the father a quick one, causes unknown, while he slept beneath a quilt made of trouser cuffs.

Body: Cut on the bias, across years. Stitch sides and shoulders, and let hang from a wire hook, diagonally.

Laka squared: her hips, her shoulders, her head, and the short straight banged wig she tugged over it. She rolled endless jelly rolls. "You look like sponge cake," Dovid said to her. "Everything you cook tastes bad." With sugar-gritty hands, she pulled his hair and shouted, "Go out to a restaurant." The twins set the table and argued over where the forks belonged. Hiding in the bathroom, Marvya made her Yo-Yo walk like a dog. Ephraim lay dead in the sitting room. The next day they would bury him.

Yaakov, the tailor-merchant, shortened trouser legs and counted silver dollars hoarded in a button chest. Customers stopped by, ordered suit coats, skimmed newspapers in the shoe department. "Ephraim used to read to me, but now he's gone," Yaakov complained. "So read yourself," answered Dovid, powdered white with lime, jerking suddenly out of the basement doorway. "My Dovid," Yaakov announced. "He's grown." Then, remembering the daily folded in his hand, he traced a line of newsprint and said, "I still can't understand this language." But in piles of weekday papers he discovered articles (with photographs) and salvaged them: wearing skimmers and floral lounge pajamas, the twins at a Brownie garden party; the twins lost on their way home from a movie theater; Dovid in a car he tried stealing; Ephraim and the way he died; Marvya in the dark with three luminous Yo-Yos; an older Marvya with a basketball.

"You're a gentle man, Yaakov," Laka said to him. "But you gave me too many of the wrong children, and I make you suffer for it."

"But I help you," he said.

"Oh, yes. You cut their fingernails."

"I'll take care of the twins," he answered. "And find the men to marry them."

But they didn't want to marry. Drancha said, "I'm going to be a nurse," packed her suitcase, and left for a hospital. "No, I won't go with her," Deeta said after Dovid suggested it. "I hate blood and white, and the dead upset me." She entered a typing pool. "Look for a man," her mother warned. "If you want a life ahead of you."

She was scared of men. On a hay ride a boy who tried to kiss her had knocked her glasses off. "You'll break them," she said.

Then seven years later a fellow merchant telephoned Yaakov. "My nephew's here, suntanned from a stay at the beach. What are your daughters up to?"

Drancha was on ward duty, Marvya on a ball court, Deeta, a twenty-three-year-old, by herself in the sitting room. "You're going," Laka told her.

She stood in the corner of the kitchen near the

wash tub. "Certainly, I'll always remember that tartan plaid dress, her prominent teeth, and those glasses. Gold-framed. What glasses," the nephew, Harmon Greenberg, later said.

"I hated him at first," Deeta said. "It was a danger signal, but despite it, we were married."

And on the wedding trip he went wild in a tunnel under the Hudson where his car stalled. When he kicked the wooden bumpers, wood chips blew in his eyes. He gritted his teeth loose. Through tears he looked at his wife and said, "Why did I ask you? I don't know why I asked you."

She answered, "But it's done with. You asked me."

Drancha married an engineer, mechanical. His name was Silverstein.

And Marvya didn't marry. "As desirable as I am," Dovid said. "Who wants her?"

But men gave her flowers as big as onions and stood on their hands and knees in front of her in the parlor. She refused them. She spun out Yo-Yos, drew them back. She dribbled basketballs. "I'm talented," she said. "I want to tour. I'll demonstrate in the aisles of department stores." Then she took a job at the five-and-dime as a night clerk and alternate cashier.

"Oh, Marvya, why not marry someone?" Yaakov asked. "Have babies."

"Please, if only for my sake," Laka said. "I'm dying."

"You? You're as healthy as a horse," Dovid told her.

But her eyes blurred, her head throbbed, her ears itched. She cooked a boiled dinner. "It's constant pain," she said. Three days later she fell over in a diabetic coma.

Deeta rushed in and cried at Laka's bedside with her year-old baby, a daughter, Ellen. Drancha arrived with her husband Bert from another city. In a white-bibbed uniform and white-winged cap, she ordered everyone out of Laka's bedroom. "You'll pay me for private duty," she told Yaakov; then to the others she said, "What Mother needs most now is quiet."

When Deeta got home, she coaxed Harmon into bed and conceived another baby.

In the projection booth in the theater where he worked, Dovid howled then switched to the second reel of a grainy pornographic movie.

Yaakov, in the kitchen, said to Bert, "At least he has a trade now. Those projectionists even let him join their union."

Laka awoke, saw cobwebs in her eyes and a white-capped shape before her. "Who are you?" she asked.

Ignoring her, Drancha leaned into the hallway. "Everyone, listen. She's snapped out of that coma."

But for months she slid in and out of it, and with each emergence, the world looked dustier. "Deeta," she said one afternoon, "Yaakov just told me. You're in your twenty-ninth week, and I didn't even know you were pregnant."

"But it doesn't show on me." Deeta lighted another cigarette. "I'm so worried about you that I can't eat anything."

"But your baby," Laka said. "What will happen to it?"

It was tiny and furry, a girl, born three days after Laka's midsummer funeral. "Named Lake," Deeta said. "In Mother's memory."

"What good does that do?" Dovid asked. "She's a baby. Mother's dead. Who'll take care of us?"

"I look to Marvya," Yaakov said, blotting his forehead with the ribbons of mourning.

But Marvya wouldn't leave her room. She sat in the dark, in the heat, in a pile of Yo-Yos. "I don't understand," she said. "Where's Mother gone? I don't want to work in the five-and-dime. I don't want to live this way."

Yaakov covered her hands with his. "Time heals. And we have to help each other."

"Ha! No, never." Gasping, she laughed at him in horrible spasms. "No, I won't slave for you, the two of you. That's what you're asking. And I won't marry a man to avoid it. Shift for yourself. Everyone for himself, do you hear me?" She pounded her walls and hurled Yo-Yos. "I won't do it. I refuse to. Do you hear me?"

"Dovid, what to do with her?" Yaakov asked.

"Have the court commit her."

Deeta and Drancha came once, but no one else visited Marvya at the state institution. "Grow up," Drancha said. "Life is hard. Face reality."

Marvya said, "Please excuse me. I have to use the bathroom."

A year later they were notified when she hanged herself from the curtain rod in the women's shower stall.

"Sick," Yaakov said. "She put herself in and out of misery."

He and Dovid, two bachelors, lived alone, ate in restaurants, and teased their waitresses. While Yaakov slept late, Dovid unlocked the store and shaking, sweating, waited on morning customers. Every night he sat sprawled alone in the bright booth off the balcony of a narrow theater. "What I know about life and love," he said, "I know from these movies."

On alternate weekends, Deeta left her husband and in her car packed her children, chickens, and pots. Laka's old kitchen warmed with reheated soup while Yaakov sucked wings and Dovid complained, "It's even worse than Mother ever made." Deeta's two girls, Ellen and Lake, cracked wishbones then riffled through trouser racks and played in the storeroom. Yaakov pried open button tins, handed out quarters. When the girls were old enough, he made them guards, watching for shoplifters. "If you spot one, signal. Use these words." Then he spoke to them in his old language.

The morning after Yaakov died, Dovid found him, his tailor's hands crusted, clutching bedclothes hand-sewn from pants scraps.

"I can't believe it," Dovid sobbed in Deeta's living room. "My only friend is gone."

"Where can Dovid live?" Deeta asked after the funeral. "He can't stay alone. If he just tried to make coffee, he'd burn himself."

"Not with me. No thank you," Drancha said. She took a train back to her husband, their family.

Deeta said, "I don't want him to, but what choice is there? Can he live with us?"

Her husband Harmon fluttered in his bedroom. "Oh, all right," he finally said. "But he has to give us something. In repayment."

Sleeves: Cut two, stitch sides, ease caps into armholes. Turn cuffs. These are hands for the pockets.

Harmon Greenberg was a sickly man who lived a convalescent life in an attic above his family: a wife, two daughters, and later, his brother-in-law, Dovid. "Men make mistakes in life," he said. "Personally, I should never have married. Stomach problems, heart problems." He patted himself. "I don't like anyone. So why should I love them?"

Bert Silverstein, son of a milkman, sent himself to college, married, and had a son and a daughter. "At least we can choose our friends," he told Drancha, "if not your family." Often he demanded things: cake, ice cream, sex, sandwiches. But on generous days he dropped coins in a salt box, and Drancha spent them on fur coats and a beach house for the children, Carl and Candy.

Inside left front pocket: Add lining and buttons.

"I'm a widow with these girls to raise," Deeta said after Harmon died and left her. "I'm thankful for my brother, who provides us with money." Then Ellen went away to school, and Deeta telephoned very early every morning. "What are you up to? Who are your boyfriends? You're my life, you and Lake. Except for both of you, I would wish, like your father, that I hadn't married."

In the kitchen Dovid spilled his milk. "Good girl," he said when Lake brought him another. "Do as he says," Deeta told her. Each week she set up folding chairs then tore tickets at the back door for his Thursday stag movies. But she mapped her days to avoid him. She ran from floor to floor; she hid in closets and behind furniture. "She's a loon," Dovid laughed. "Like our Marvya." Nearby with a heavy-healed shoe in her hand, Lake wanted to slay him. From a crack in a door, she watched him clean his toes with a knife while he cried over radio melodrama.

"What Dovid wants, I anticipate," Deeta said. She ran to him with hot dogs, comics, hash-browned potatoes. "I do it for money, for both of us, Lake." Then rubbing her hips, she complained of arthritis.

And Ellen never came home again. "I know better than that," she wrote Lake in a letter. They never learned what happened to her, though Deeta thought she married a lawyer.

Recommended fabric: Winter worsted, but in the left pocket, slip a scrap of tropical.

When arthritic Deeta fell from a ladder and died, only Dovid and Lake troubled to bury her. "Where are the others?" Dovid asked. His feet slid and kicked gravel down the path at the cemetery. "But Lake's here. My Lake. You'll take care of me?"

"No."

And she disappeared to a warmer part of what once was called the new continent.

Afterword of Dovid Shromm, survivor, a palsied man in worsted top-stitched sport clothes: pants, pocketed gown, and skimpy over vest. He lives in a black room, an album lined with photographs (see drawing and caption, back of pattern envelope): So this is what she makes of us. That crazy girl. Who knows what happened to her. But she asked for it, when she left us. We're her family.

Note from Lake, stapled to the flap of the pattern envelope: Though the fabric tears, unravels, you can't forget things. You can never run away. They're behind me; they are with me. I am wearing them. They're my family.

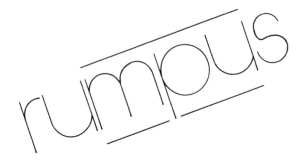

rumpus

hings happened to Janet. Things
happened to people she knew. It all
was the stuff of life: money, illness,
and melodrama. Now that she finished her tale, she jiggled her
daughter on her lap. When she and Jack went out, they liked to
bring their daughter. In the room people said, "I can't believe the
man died. . . . And his mother . . . His poor wife . . . To think they're
Janet's cousins . . . No, she said just friends of cousins . . .
Amazing . . . Horrible . . . ." And Janet, though she had lived this
tale and felt this tale and even twice before told this tale, was

weighted again by the injustice of it. Her mouth turned down.
Her eyes swelled, enhancing her beauty, which was all eyes,
really. "Here, Trinka." Once more, deftly, she jiggled and
distracted her daughter, who wanted an almond from the box of
nuts. "The doctor says you can't digest those yet. Moo-cow, darling.
Fish-face?" Janet puckered. "I think our hostess has a treat in
store. Hungry? Yes?"

Trinka nodded. She had not liked the cheese and
crackers or the eggplant spread; she had not liked the salad with
olives in it; she had not liked the chicken in sauce; she had no
taste for rice; and her doctor forbade her nuts. If there was ice
cream, though . . . . She studied the room with sober eyes, and
everyone watched and imagined her thoughts. Earlier her shrieks
had been ignored, but silent, she drew attention to herself. Now it
seemed this was a party for the child.

"Oh, Trinka, here we go!" Janet spoke. "Isn't that
right, Daddy?"

"Right on it. Would you look at that," Jack, the
impish father, said.

The others had no children yet and were loath to
encourage poor nutrition. But with Trinka they, too, leaned toward
the fudge ice cream packed in parfait glasss, and they wanted
some.

Lynn, their hostess, said, "I counted one each, but
I've got more frozen." In the living room she set the ice cream tray
atop her desk, beside the ripened cheese and cracker plate.
"I forgot to clear this off. Last call. Anybody?"

"When there's sweets?" Janet asked, and laughed.

"Well, then," Lynn said, "better grab a glass before
it melts."

Everyone lined up. Janet came with Trinka on her
hip. She spoke to her child; she spoke to the woman nearest them.
"Eileen, I meant to ask, how's your sister? . . . Yes, Trinket, we're
next. . . . Is she really? Back to college? . . . Yes, darling, you and
Mommy will split an ice cream." She encompassed every moment,

or did she shrink some of them? Whatever, she herself was always there, complete.

Later, she stood by the kitchen stove, one of four women gathered, old friends in an apartment in Wilmington, their hometown. Eileen and Kay, like Janet, now lived elsewhere and this week, or weekend, were visiting their parents. Only Lynn had moved back to Wilmington after college. "Janet," she said, "are you sure Trinka wouldn't like a pillow? Would she be happier in the bedroom, do you think?"

Janet faintly shook her head no. She was eavesdropping on Jack, lulling Trinka to sleep in the living room. For a moment her friends listened, too. "Jack's telling a bedtime joke," Janet explained. "The punch line comes soon. It's not too bad."

"Does he still make funny movies?" Eileen asked. "Didn't he, when you were going out?"

"Just one. I think I sent you photographs of the opening, at some restaurant. You might not believe it, but now he's collecting railway passenger cars."

"You're kidding!"

"But where do you put them?"

"He rents space in a railroad yard."

"Is there money in that?"

Janet laughed and gaily flicked a burner on and off. Lynn said, "Be careful."

"Sorry."

"Janet, I meant to tell you that Trinket's even more adorable than last time."

"Thank you, Kay. Our little Trinket-Bauble."

"And Jack is great with her," Lynn added.

"Listen," Eileen said, "Jack is great, period. Charming, daring . . . ."

"Well . . . ," Janet smiled. "That can bring us trouble sometimes. Aside from being husband, father, lawyer, he's a character. But I agree, he's wonderful."

The three others smiled, too, happy for Janet who had a husband and a baby to extoll. At her wedding in Denver, the three had glimpsed then what lay ahead ready-made for her: Jack's family, Jack's clique, Jack's quirks, Jack's town. Jack was taking her. And yet she remained herself, up to the last tending to friends, introducing older and newer, connecting them. *Lynn, that problem with your wrist circulation, well Sarah — we met at U. Colorado — Sarah suffers too! Sarah, this is Lynn.* Minutes before the procession, she stood fanning her nails dry in the vestibule outside the chapel. Her father, suddenly ill, had been hospitalized in Wilmington. Her mother and brother had travelled to Denver alone. Her father might die. She smoothed her hair. She grabbed her bouquet. The music began. Her nails were sticky. Her brother came and walked her down the aisle.

And she was beautiful. Through the ceremony, each of the three had imagined herself in Janet's place with a blank-faced man, and tonight, years later, the face of the man was still blank for all three. But there were men, and the three had jobs. Their lives they described in a sentence or two. Janet led listeners through paragraphs. Janet was Janet. Eileen, Lynn, and Kay, as if X, Y, and Z, were part of a different experiment.

But they'd shared girlhoods in Wilmington, and now they laughed at that curse. "It was horrible, wasn't it?" As adults they saw the place simply as a place, like any other.

"Sections are lovely," Eileen said. "I guess I was too miserable to know it then. Remember?"

All around, giggles briefly surged and fell.

Lynn said, "Well, I got that job, so I moved back. And I soon found it wasn't bad at all." She stood taller, justified, silent but, if asked, ready to detail an average twenty-four hours: leave bed, dress, go to work — she was a teacher — swim late afternoon in an indoor pool, prepare and devour dinner, plan the next day's class, go out sometimes, take enrichment courses, then back to bed. On purpose she exhausted herself.

"I guess it might be kind of fun. Oh, pardon. . . ."

Kay interrupted herself with a yawn. Always she'd been fuzzy-voiced. As though recently roused in the middle of the day, at odd times she would stretch her limbs and crack her bones. In her twenties, she became more aware of these oddities. "Hmm? What? What did I miss?" She chanted the old refrain that had carried down the corridors in high school. Her laughter spurred the others. Hilarious! But her daze was sexy now. Even leaning against the sharp edge of a kitchen counter, she looked utterly relaxed and comfortable.

Eileen, crushed too near the refrigerator handle, shifted a bit. Since the others recalled her miseries of old, she would spare them the latest of the same sort. She envied Kay her airiness, Lynn her intent and severity. And Janet? She stared and Janet noticed her and said, "Don't be glum 'Leen. Are you tired?"

"Oh, you know me," Eileen answered. Then she rolled her eyes. "Naturally despondent. Sadness suffused me in the womb. I was born sad."

They roared at this, like old times.

Janet said, "Here's an idea. Let's go out together, to a bar!"

The others wondered, had they ever been to a bar together?

"Not that your party's not fantastic, Lynn, but this . . . ," Janet paused. "This would be just the four of us again."

"But it's just the four of us now," Lynn said.

"Standing in your kitchen?" Janet glanced around. "How festive. Come on, Lynn. Jack will baby-sit Trinket if I ask."

Kay said, "I go to bars a lot."

Lynn said, "I've been to them."

Meanwhile, Janet poked her head into the living room and called out "Jack!" in a harsh whisper.

Lynn touched her arm. "Janet, please. . . ."

"Please me," Jack said. "Please? Now that I'm reunited with the grown-up ladies." He stood beside the sofa where Trinka lay, arms and legs flung wide, as though she had fallen asleep while sky diving.

"Isn't Trinka sweet," Kay said. "Now, what does her daddy want?"

"An audience. Wait till you hear my jokes." Jack tapped his eyeglasses. "When I take these off, the nose comes, too. Or how about a parlor game? Charades? We'll act out incidents from Janet's life. Lynn and 'Leen, perk up. Scared of me?"

Lynn loudly drew in breath. "Of course not."

Eileen said, "I think I'm scared of everything."

"Are you badgering my friends, dear?" Janet swerved close to Jack and bumped her head to his. She was just his height. "I don't mean to interrupt, but he's my husband, you know? . . . Dear darling, would you take Trinket back to her grandmother's?"

"Daddy do! Then where does he meet you? Have you heard? We're performing your life."

"Darling . . . ."

The three friends sidled toward the kitchen to let husband and wife settle things between themselves. Perhaps for charades they would try to recreate this scene: Janet and Jack argue playfully, with witnesses. Or would they start far back? Janet's "older" parents meet and marry late in life. A son and a daughter are born. Classmates visit. Open the door to whiffs of melon rind and chicken bones. Mother offers toll house cookies on a turquoise plate. Kindly father reads in the den with the book on his belly. Brother thumps upstairs, slams shut a door. Janet emerges in furry flat-soled slippers and leads guests to the cellar for Ping-Pong. She loses baby fat. She grows her hair far past her shoulders. She dates boys. She leaves for college. Of the four friends, enrolled in four scattered schools, she is the one who visits, who carries a backpack, who sleeps on the floor. The other three could never capture her matter-of-fact solicitude. Now as then, she comes first, but she has time left for them.

And so she turned. "All arranged. Daddy leaves with daughter."

"Into the sunset. Never to be seen again," Jack

said. He cradled Trinka low. Her hair brushed his belt. Over his left arm, her calves swayed. "Remember you asked for this, Janet. My lawyer will get in touch."

"Mine, too."

They kissed with their child suspended between them.

"So this is married life," Kay said, wistfully. "It's precious. Just what I've dreamed of. But not for me."

"Kay, don't! None of you!" Janet sprang past Trinka and Jack toward the three women who stood in a solemn row barring the way to the kitchen. "You're not spinsters yet. If only I could find men to marry you."

"Oh, well," Kay said.

"You sound like my mother," Eileen said.

Lynn said, "I'm not going out drinking. It's too late."

"Aren't we playing charades?" Kay asked.

"That was a joke." Janet smiled. "Now Kay, you never really thought . . . ."

"Ahem," Jack said. "Man and babe clear out before catfight. Besides, I can't maintain this grip much longer. Ta-ta, ladies. Many thanks, Lynn. The front door, Janet? And then assistance at the car?"

Janet saluted. "My duty, sir." Trinka murmured; her foot ticked the second; the buckle on her shoe strap glinted in the light. "See," Janet told her friends, "you're not missing anything."

Eileen said, "You mean we miss it all. But that's not right. We have our pleasures."

"I'll bet," Jack said.

Janet said, "I let my husband leer, and he lets me. Come on, darling." She extended an arm and guided her family toward the front door and out to the first floor foyer. With a thud, the building's main door swung to, then back.

Lynn said, "Can't we meet tomorrow? Let's all say good night. I have a feeling I might cry soon."

"Lynn, don't." Kay swooped to hug her. "Please don't."

Eileen moved closer, too. "It'll be fun. You'll see. Just the four of us again."

Outside, Janet's heels tapped on the street. Sounds came through the window, but words were indistinguishable. A motor started.

"Think how many nights we spend alone," Eileen said.

"If you're worried about cleaning up," Kay said, "I'll be back here tomorrow, bright and early, to help."

"No. Thanks." Lynn steadied herself and pulled away. "You're right. We'll go out now and get it over with."

"Listen to how much fun she is!" Kay squeezed Lynn's shoulders again, for a moment. "We're getting you drunk, we're getting you drunk, we're getting you . . . ."

"Well we won't force it down your throat," Eileen said. "Calm down, Kay-bird."

"No, Kay-bird, sing out! I'm free for the night!" It was Janet's voice. The others, in their huddle, turned to see her peering through the doorway. "Where to? Hurry up."

"My car," Eileen offered. "It doesn't matter where for now. Let's just get out."

"Agreed!" Kay said. She pretended to capture Lynn and drag her into the chilly night. "Of course you have your keys. That table lamp's on, and I saw you fasten the window shut. 'Leen, where's your car?"

"This way," Eileen said.

Janet scanned the block expectantly. "Will we dance tonight?" she asked. "Whose father's taking, whose picks up? We'll be late. I love that perfume. What brand? Who went heavy on mouthwash?"

Kay said, "You remember."

Janet said, "Of course I do."

"The lucky forget," Eileen said. "Here's the vehicle."

She drove swiftly on empty streets, toward the highway and the local bars.

"We might be the only four awake in Wilmington,"
Kay joked. "But there's bound to be people at the bar. If we're
pestered, then what?"

"As your chaperone," Janet said, "I'll throw you to
the wolves."

At last Eileen slowed and signaled to turn at a busy
intersection, four lanes and a string of hamburger stands,
supermarkets, bars. She asked, "Should we drink at a bowling
alley? We can, you know."

"For God's sake!"

"Anywhere but . . . ."

"I have a headache already."

"All right. Point made. Beachcomber? With the
totem poles out front?"

"What's wrong with you?"

"Here's something. Rumpus Room." And she
signalled to turn again.

They parked and climbed cement steps to the
door. Inside, a narrow flight cleated with aluminum led down
again. The railing shook. Lynn asked, "Is this a basement or what?"

Kay said, "It looked like a box from the parking lot."

All around the room, on ledges high up, were
sporting trophies: bowlers, golfers, baseball players captured
midgame and fastened to pedestals by the foot. On each table was
a trophy cup. No one sat at the tables. Two men, on stools at the
bar, watched a television bolted to a shelf. The bartender called
out, "Right with you, ladies. Take a seat. Your choice."

They hesitated. Kay raised her brows, Lynn covertly
shook her head, Eileen grimaced, Janet mocked her. These were
gestures meant for threshholds: should we enter? But they had
already. Janet said, "Why not?" and they followed her to a table
away from the bar, in a paneled corner.

"Scatter toys, add a washer-dryer, and this is nearly
our basement," Janet said. "Except our bar is smaller."

"Really?"

"You have a bar?"

They settled in and chattered about the trophies, all unengraved because no one had really won them. "There's a store downtown that sells these things," Lynn said. "And plush toys, too."

Kay glanced again at the figurines. "So that's how they got them. I wondered. Has this place been here long? It's creepy. But wait, no." She shook her head as the others turned, ready to seize their handbags from their laps and flee. "We're here. Let's stay. And look, the bartender's coming."

"He resembles that old chem teacher," Janet said. "What was his name?"

Smiling, neat in cardigan, shirt, and tie, he ambled toward them. "Well, girls, what'll it be?"

"Are you Mr. McGowan?" Janet asked.

"No, I'm not. All decided?" He chose Kay first. "How about it?"

"Yes, thanks. A glass of red wine."

Eileen watched for his nod. "A bottle of beer. Something local."

"Sure thing."

"Do you have ginger ale?" Lynn asked.

"Sorry, the closest is tonic."

"Oh, Lynn," Kay urged, "have something stronger."

"Please, Kay . . . ." And then, "Tonic water is fine."

Janet still deliberated. "Oh, oh, vodka on ice with chartreuse."

"We've got vodka, we've got ice . . . ."

"Then surprise me. Vodka on ice with something bright stirred in." As she watched him walk off, Janet hunched down to whisper. "I wonder what he'll bring. . . . Oh, by the way," her voice rose, "may I share my summer party treat? Chocolate ice cream blended with crème de menthe."

"Do you entertain a lot?" Lynn asked.

"Always. Jack has his old crowd, from school."

She brightened a bit. "Imagine if we still lived near each other!"

The others brightened, too. Then their drinks arrived, and Janet brandished a folder of traveller's checks. "Let me. I have to spend these."

Eileen reached for Janet's arm. "Come on, they keep."

"I know that, silly. Who's got a pen? Or how about one giant bill before we leave?" Janet turned to the bartender, who just then was wiping at the table with a thin cotton rag. "How's that?"

"Fine, ma'am."

"To Friendship!" Janet said, setting up the echo. The friends bumped their odd-shaped glasses and laughed. The bartender vanished. They toasted again: "Togetherness and Staying in Touch!"

"Oh, I want to give us a party!" For a moment Janet squeezed shut her eyes. "My parties are fun. But you wouldn't believe some we go to. Caterers, for a handful of couples. When I phone out for pizza, everyone says, 'Isn't that quaint.' Food's their latest thing. A hobby, sort of. No more drugs. The wives are getting pregnant now. There, at least, I was first, and I have the daughter and the abdomen to show for it."

"You're so far ahead of us," Lynn said. "And really, you look great."

"I like to dress up and eat at fancy restaurants sometimes," Kay admitted. "Is that what you mean?"

Janet nodded. "That's them, but every week. And we can't keep up. We can't." She drank on, and then she said, "You're friends. I'll let you have it straight."

"Oh, yes," Kay said.

"We'd tell you," Eileen said, "but what's to tell?"

Janet stared at the damp rings on the table and trailed her finger through one. "All right." She looked up. "Here it is. We live beyond our means. We're in way over our heads. Jack has problems with cash flow."

"Really?"

"Sorry."

"It must be hard."

In the pseudo-basement gloom, the three muttered and then said nothing for a while. Lynn sighed and breathed the beery mist airborne as Eileen decanted from bottle to mug. *Over their heads:* the words stuck. "Janet," Lynn begged, "you're happy, aren't you?"

"Of course we are. But some nights there's nothing in the freezer or my purse, and I've already stolen the last coins dropped in Trinka's silver donkey bank. So I phone friends. I tell them, 'Bring the steak. I'll cook it. I'll clean up.' And they come. For a couple of weeks last winter it went on like that."

"Sounds like fun." Kay spoke in a quaver. "Like a grab bag."

"Preferable to tuna and noodles from the cupboard," Eileen added. "Have you ever thought of omelets? They can be good stuffed with vegetables or cheese . . . ."

"Eggs are breakfast," Janet announced. "Besides, Jack only eats them out, Saturdays at the crossroads diner. You wouldn't believe, when my mother visited, the way she carried on. 'You have eggs here. Why's he going out? Can't you toast bread? Can't you brew coffee?' Of course I could, or he could. For a year in college he worked as a short order cook, the year his father disowned him temporarily. He took turns disowning everybody. But all eight kids got money when he died."

"What a family," Kay said.

Janet said, "They're crazy." Then she swung her arms to attract the barman's attention. "Bring more! Another round!"

Jack doesn't want eight children, I hope, or does he?" Eileen asked.

"Four," Janet answered. "I'm pushing for three. He claims our genes are too good to control."

Kay shook her head. "I wouldn't want eight."

"His mother didn't; his father did. You see who won. And now there are so many presents to give. Birthdays, holidays. His baby sister got engaged, and twelve people honored her at twelve different showers. That meant twelve gifts, plus wedding and engagement."

"You're kidding."

"That's ridiculous."

"We didn't have food, and we owed gifts, and the mortgage, and payments on the cars. . . ."

"But Janet," Eileen said, "what in the world will you do? How did you get money for traveller's checks?"

"Let me finish. Jack's practice goes up and down, and now it's up. . . . Oh, thanks," Janet said to the bartender, "that was quick."

"To Jack's practice," Lynn proposed, and glasses touched haphazardly.

"Does he need any help in his office?" Kay asked.

Janet said, "Are you looking for work?"

"No, but you . . . ." Kay paused. "Could you help him? Or get some other kind of job?"

"And who would care for Trinka the way I do?" Janet studied her glass. "You know, I think this is vodka and food coloring."

Lynn said, "How horrible."

"But I'm drunk. It's done the trick."

"Janet," Eileen asked, "didn't you like that job you had, before Trinka?"

"I had two jobs," Janet said. "Remember, in my first month of married life, my father died and I was fired. Probably because I'd planned the wedding from my desk, renting tents, calling caterers—for a wedding they're okay—deciding on a rock 'n' roll band from tapes. They would play me their tapes over the phone."

Kay said, "That band you hired was wonderful."

"And then your father died," Eileen said.

"Yes. And to my boss a funeral only meant more time off. So he gave me all the time in the world. Day after day, I sat on our bed, hating him and crying. Jack understood. The year before his own father had died. He said, 'You've got to get out there, Janet.' So I got another job. I liked it enough."

"And now?" Lynn asked.

"My job is Trinka. But it's not a job. She's so important, I can't tell you. Jack knows it, too. We're carrying on. When my father couldn't talk anymore, that was the message he scrawled on a tablet page. 'Carry on.'"

"Oh, Janet, you'll make us weep," Kay said.

"You don't miss a career?" Lynn asked.

"A career? That's money," Janet said. "And Trinket's life." She sat straight and bleary-eyed, her arms on the table. "Life," she repeated, as though her friends kept it from themselves.

I t was a long way for an old man. He had
searched half an hour for a meter and
had at last found one part-way down
the hill on Powell. He knew it was wrong to leave a car like his at
a meter; it stood so high above the others that it practically begged
to be stolen or maimed. Someone might easily pry the filigree
doe—his emblem—off the grille, snap the antenna, puncture the
tires. . . . But mightn't that happen even in a costly garage? And
there, the owner himself could be killed en route to the elevator.
Perhaps he should hire a chauffeur to circle city blocks with

equanimity. In due time. Now he must keep in mind where he'd parked. He chose a sofa in the hotel's lobby and settled down to appréciate a mustachioed young man. *Would you like a job?* Past the draperies and palms, he saw into the bar where a pianist dressed as a bellhop played and sang a horrid medley on and on. He looked out the glass to California Street. Would the broker revolve in, or tug at the hefty side door? He would soon find out; he must be patient. Meanwhile he had fifteen minutes to catch his breath.

Hello, Paul. And he would extend his hand, not to be shaken but held for however long. *Hello, Rand.* Again he put his own name and a greeting in the mouth he did not know. *Hello, Rand.* Rand: a kind of money, appropriately. All the brokers and venturers nagged rich Rand Waldhorn, who bought sometimes, but not usually. Only as a lark had he consented to meet broker Paul, to savor in the flesh those deep "indeeds" at the end of his sentences.

After aging and aging, Rand's own timbre had become more conventional. Men who survived long years often endured a second change of voice, to high plaintiveness. But Rand's voice had never really changed, so it did not have to revert.

"Mr. Waldhorn? I'm Paul Hamilton."

"Paul! You're early." Rand Waldhorn took a moment to boost himself up from the sofa cushions. He held out his hand to be nursed, and Paul Hamilton pumped as though to resuscitate. "How very good to meet you, Paul. You must have climbed off that billboard overhanging the highway on my drive in. You're terribly handsome." Rand grinned. Had he shocked Paul? No, surely Paul knew the common knowledge about Waldhorn in the Bay Area. Now Paul half glanced at Rand, half glanced away, like one of those stern men advertising neckties, whiskey, cologne, luggage. . . .

"Where shall we go, Paul? The bar?"

"Sounds good."

"They had music earlier, but now it's stopped. Oh,

look, there's the pianist greeting his consort, El Mustachio. Well, to the bar?"

They walked through the lobby toward lengths of fringed blue-velvet draperies tied back here and there to create entrances. The bar was darker; the palms grew thicker.

"In the hotel across the street, I think, the bar is a rain forest. It drizzles indoors. You just watch, though. You needn't get wet."

"Would you rather go there?"

"No, no, Paul. It's nice here. Let's grab this table, hmm?"

"I got word earlier this afternoon on Baystrand. And the prospects look excellent, aside from rumors you may have heard."

"Oh, yes, the partnership." Rand slid across the banquette, and Paul pulled out a bamboo chair. "I'm not buying, Paul. Perhaps I should have told you over the phone, but I couldn't. I'd hoped you might outline other schemes today. Besides, a chat was in order and . . . . My, you look fit in your clothes. I feel miniscule in this suit. Are they still wearing double-breasted? Good heavens, I'm associating you again with that haberdashery billboard. Forgive me, Paul."

"What other investments were you thinking of?"

"Just let me cogitate a minute. Meanwhile, you can tell me if you live alone."

"If I what?" And then immediately Paul calmed himself, perhaps with the vision of a sum of money and a possible deal. "Mr. Waldhonr, I'll tell you if you're adamant, though otherwise . . . ."

"No, certainly, Paul. But I do hope you're happy."

Rand also hoped he lived alone, if only to spare any less beautiful human being, man or woman, from awaiting his return to dinners shrinking in a warm oven or chilling on the table in an unlit room. *Where is he now, and who's with him? I just can't stand this anymore. He said 6:30, and it's 8:00. He wants me only for my income, damn him. . . .*

"Mr. Waldhorn?"

"Yes?"

"Are you ill or distracted or . . . ." Paul's brows conferred in worry. The planes of his high cheeks seemed to shift beneath his skin. His face was in earnest, and every perfectly imperfect feature asked after Rand: his long, fine nose, his plumped mouth, the niche between the swell of his lower lip and the jut of his chin. ". . . Mr. Waldhorn?"

"I'm very well, and please call me Rand. Now that we're friends." Now that they were almost sharing confidences. *It's that bad at home, Paul? Keeps tabs on you! Money fights! But don't wrinkle up so. I think I can help.* Again Rand watched Paul's brows huddle, to fret this time over sales, commissions, dollars and cents.

". . . in your tax bracket."

"Yes, yes, you're absolutely right, Paul."

They each could console the other this afternoon. *Just once. Or else again and again, if you insist, Paul! But remember, once will do. And then back you go, with all your tags in place.* Rand's sister used beaded evening purses in a similar fashion, with the tags and strings clasped inside. She used them once and then returned them for a refund, though God knew she could afford to buy them and throw them away.

". . . investment needs," Paul concluded. "I'm sure of it."

"You're very right, and you must remind me to leave you my sister's name, as another prospect. But first, Paul, please order me some kind of drink. I see our waiter is finally on his way, though when he gets here, I'll be heading for the men's room. . . . No, don't bother to stand, Paul, thank you."

Rand tottered off, giving Paul a chance to escape. It was only fair. But would Paul leave or not? Would he? And so Rand bedeviled himself.

In the corridor he passed the men's room door and lingered by the jeweler's window for distraction. He might buy that bug brooch for his sister, Janette, in honor of the long, long roaches that eventually infested every Waldhorn bakeshop. Yesterday at lunch, he and Janette had opened all her coffers, and she owned nothing like this. Maybe Paul dealt in diamonds and gold.

He turned from the brooch and realized he had led himself in an arc and now stood near an obscure entrance to the bar. He might go in this way and surprise Paul, if Paul had waited for him. He squinted through a dazzle of strung glass beads, and saw that Paul had *indeed.* He must coax that word out of him. He watched Paul aim his profile toward the parted draperies and glower, as though he expected an opponent to emerge from there. But tricky Rand was coming in roundabout, through the jangling beads.

"What is your sport, Paul?" Rand spoke to the man's shoulders; the man jerked, but then in no time righted himself. "I didn't mean to startle you."

"Not at all. Soccer." Paul tilted his glass and smiled, as though happy with a private, wicked joke. "Glad to see you. I was beginning to worry. I'd guess you like golf."

"I swim." Rand eased himself down. "You've been amusing yourself?"

"No. I ordered you scotch."

"You shouldn't have told me! The game is for me to close my eyes and bring the elixir to my lips. But never mind. Do you know about jewelry? No? Nor do I. My family made money with pastry, and I made much more out of money itself. But then, you're conversant with my reputation as financial gambler?"

"I am indeed."

"Oh, thank you, Paul." Rand touched Paul's wrist lightly, with his fingertips. In his school days, girls had shrieked when he touched them like that, as a prank, of course. "Am I creepy? That's what my sister's friends told me. You shake your head. No? Come with me upstairs, Paul."

"If that's what you want."

"How kind! I was so frightened to meet you, you won't believe. He'll be beautiful, I thought, and I'm an old furrowed. . . ."

"If we're going, let's go."

"But mustn't we have a plan? Who checks in?"

"You."

"I still can't fathom it. Imagine! This miser with Adonis on Nob Hill!"

"Come off it, you're not a miser, Rand. I'll look for you once you've got the key. How much do you think it will cost?"

"Well over a hundred, perhaps two. Wait by the elevators, Paul. Would you like a suite? Bidet?"

"Go."

"Dear boy, I can tell you're going to break my heart."

Secretly, in his pocket, Rand held the key, hooked to a flat brass charm engraved with a room number. An elevator opened, and a courteous couple tried to detain it for him. "Oh, no, thank you, I'm waiting for a friend." Just then he glimpsed Paul crossing the lobby from the bar. He had not bothered to button his blazer, which fanned his pale-blue shirt front slightly. He saw Rand and immediately looked away, as if casing the lobby for a more likely date. Or perhaps he had scrambled off a billboard to film commercials in the Mark Hopkins. They'd promoted him from stills. Today's script: defy that old gawker and exit via the revolving door. Outside in the horseshoe driveway a pretty woman awaits.

But he did not leave. He stepped with Rand into the very next elevator car.

"Aren't you with the dentistry convention, too?" Rand asked. "Dr. Hamilton? I think we're on the same floor. Twenty-five?"

"Yes indeed," Paul said.

The room reeked of jonquils and overlooked both

the Bay Bridge and the Golden Gate. "What flowers! And two beds! More than I'd bargained for." Rand began to bear down on the nearest bed with both hands. "I used to love to go to Sloane's and test out mattresses. I'm at it again, practically doing push-ups here. Do you travel much?" Rand straightened his back and stared at Paul, who stood in a chilly pose beside the bureau. Now he was the one with secrets, while Rand skittered along on talk.

"Did I mention my companion to you, Paul? The travel writer, Henry Harrison? When he's in one place, we live together, so you see I'm not so desperate. But Henry won't be jealous. Now and then he permits this old man . . . ."

"Exactly how old are you? Let me see your driver's license."

"Must I? The photograph is wretched. But your hand implores. I'll just feel in here . . . ." Groping inside his suit coat, Rand managed several awkward steps. "Nifty hiding place, but I can never . . . . Ah, got it now." When he touched the leather, he wished that he himself were as smooth-skinned. And what of Paul? "How much money would you like, my boy? Let me choose the bills. No? Another shake of your head." Rand held the billfold out and expected Paul to search it, strip it, and give it back. Instead Paul dropped it in his blazer pocket.

"You know, Waldhorn, you've really inconvenienced me today. You intended to."

"But Paul, you mustn't think . . . . Avengings don't occur between friends. Won't you give me my credit cards? They're tucked in a little slot. Oh, Paul, Paul, Paul. I see my saying your name profanes it for you. Please, Paul, don't leave. The bank card's fuchsia. Just give me that. Fuchsia, puce, lilac, azure! Is that what you'd like to hear from this old . . . ."

The door slammed, and Rand Waldhorn sat down alone on a tapestried bed.

In the lobby half an hour later, Rand told the desk clerk he had lost his wallet and had searched the suite without luck. If the wallet should appear, would someone telephone him in Mill Valley? He was upset and could not wait for the house detective. Anyway, the loss was accidental and not a crime.

As he descended the hill to his meter, he felt that he was tall and shrinking steadily, until he became himself again. No one accosted him. The car was fine, unticketed, unharmed.

Henry leaned over the upstairs balustrade. "I heard your car, Rand. How'd it go? You look exhausted."

Rand stood in the entranceway and blankly glanced up. He had no umbrella to return to the stand, no hat to dangle from his choice of pegs, no desire to examine his face in the oak-framed mirror.

"That suit has outgrown you since you wore it last," Henry said. "Did you enter the partnership?"

"No, it was a rook. I knew it all along, but I wanted to meet the broker. He was better than I could have hoped. The image of the man who models men's wear on those billboards. You know, the scuffed one with the bandaid on his cheek. We went upstairs, and he rolled me."

"Good lord, are you hurt?"

"I'm feeling fine, for an ancient adolescent. Robbery is a sort of thrill, innocent and . . . ."

"Oh, before it slips my mind, Janette called."

"I have one of her watches."

"She thought so. She said to keep it."

"I will."

"Rand, are you sure you're not hurt?"

"Well, of course he hurt my feelings. Will you be working late?"

"Probably. I have . . . ."

"Yes, yes. Go back to work."

He had amassed his fortune under constraint, and then the world had relaxed. He had so much freedom now. He lay fully dressed on the daybed in his room. This was not the connubial chamber; that was another, and each man had his own besides. How perfect was their house: austere furnishings, real art, a deck with a view of their pool and of deer feeding on the hillside shrubbery, everywhere shelves of biographies whose subjects they dared to speak of as acquaintances. *Do you know what Edith Wharton did in Paris in nineteen* . . . . Perhaps he should call Janette.

His wallet would be found, he thought. Shredded and unidentifiable. Leather, plastic, cash: so much confetti in a brown paper bag.

Tomorrow he would seek out aging women who had everything, and they would sit in the shade and bemoan together.

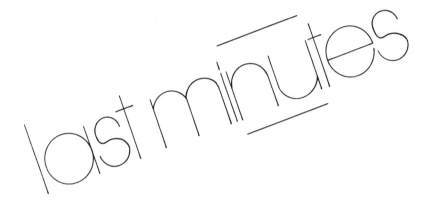

last minutes

was fifteen on the fifteenth. My father died on the first, my grandmother on the twelfth, my boyfriend on the eighteenth. "You're next," my mother said to me on the twenty-second. She handed me a pack of razor blades and a blue revolver. "I suggest the revolver," she whispered, "but either way, do me a favor and crawl into a plastic bag first." She opened the basement door and waved. "Good-by, Dena."

In the basement I used the laundry room phone and called a friend of mine.

"She's not here," her brother said.

I dialed again.

"Didn't I just tell you she's not here?"

"I'm desperate," I said. "I'm going to kill myself."

"But she's not here."

I called my mother upstairs.

"Terrified?" she asked. "Just relax and get on with it."

"I'm too cold to."

"Hold on a minute."

She opened the door and threw down some blankets. "Better?" she asked when she picked up the phone again.

"I'm thirsty now."

"Well, there's running water right next to you, isn't there?"

"I don't want water. I want . . . ."

"You want, you want, you always want. Why don't you kill yourself and leave me alone already?"

She hung up on me.

I called my sister at her college.

"She's in the bathroom," her roommate said.

"It's important."

"She'll call you back."

"No, I'll wait."

I waited ten minutes.

"What the hell do you want?" my sister asked.

"How many times do I have to tell you that I call home on Thursdays. Don't call me on Wednesday when I'm calling home on Thursday."

"I need to talk to you."

"Does Mother know you're calling? It's such a waste of money. It's ridiculous. I should be studying."

"I'm going to kill myself."

"I can't believe this. Dena, if there hasn't been enough death this month, even that asshole you were going out with . . . ."

"He wasn't an asshole."

"He was an asshole. Asshole, asshole," she said, then disconnected me.

I dialed cousin Richard who once said I could depend on him.

"Forget it this time," Richard said.

I called his sister Brenda.

"Dena who?" Brenda asked.

I called my mother again.

"You mean you're still alive? Dena, I sent you down there hours ago."

I dialed Information. Information said to dial 0.

I dialed 0.

0 said, "Dial H-O-T-L-I-N-E."

I dialed H-O-T-L-I-N-E.

"Hello, Hotline."

"Help," I said. "I'm going to kill myself."

"Aw don't," Hotline said. "Aw don't. Aw don't. Aw don't . . . ."

I dialed my mother again.

"I knew it was you," she said. "Who else would wake me?"

"I'm sorry."

"Tell me one thing, are you in the bag yet?"

"No."

"Dena, what have you been doing with yourself? Get on with it. And if you expect to be noisy, turn on the washing machine first."

I undressed then stuffed my clothes and blankets into the washing machine. I sprinkled soap on top of them. I turned the knob to the warm setting and dropped the lid down.

After I found a plastic trash bag, I shook it open and crawled inside, taking the weapons and the phone with me. I picked the receiver up. "Daddy?"

"Listen to your mother," he answered. "I don't

care what you do. Just keep your distance. After all, I died to get away from you."

"Is Granny with you?"

"Yes," she said. "What's that noise I hear? Is the washer running? And why don't you hurry up and slit your wrists or whatever? A woman my age can't put up with your nonsense. By the way, how's your sister doing?"

"Fine," my sister said. "And I miss you."

"Do it with the revolver," my boyfriend said. "Stick it in your mouth and point it toward the ceiling."

"Mother!"

"Dena, how many times do I have to tell you," my mother said.

"But it's so hot in here."

"You're hot, you're cold. What's wrong with you?"

"Don't tell me she's given herself a fever," Granny said.

"Dena, this is Mother. Does your head hurt?"

"Yes."

"Then keep her away from me," my father said.

"We were going to break up anyway," my boyfriend said.

"Did you twist the bag shut? Twist the bag shut," my mother said. "Or I'll have a mess on my hands. Bring the edges to the inside and twist the goddamn bag shut."

"But Mother, it's even hotter now."

"Breathe deeply, Dena, as if you felt nauseated."

"I can't. The walls are closing in on me," I said.

"The walls are closing in on her," they said.

"Please, the plastic's sticking to me."

No one answered.

white boy

S he had first seen him wearing sweat socks bunched down between the first and second toes of each foot to accommodate black rubber thongs. She associated this foot garb vaguely and incorrectly with an Eastern religion. She noticed he was prettier than she. He was nice to her because he was nice, and she imagined many beautiful women he'd been even nicer to.

They were next door neighbors on the second story of an oblong efficiency apartment house. Often from her sofa she watched him clomp along the outdoor catwalk that rimmed the second story and linked the twin outdoor staircases. When he passed her windows he looked straight ahead. When she passed his she pretended to survey the parking lot. In quest of a dime he once came to her door clutching ten pennies, and she asked him inside.

It turned out he had no telephone. He'd been on his way to the booth at the nearest gas station. "No telephone?" she said, suddenly embarrassed that she had one.

"I've heard yours ringing," he said.

"How annoying."

"Not at all. May I use it sometime?"

"Peter, of course."

"Now?"

"Yes, but . . . ." She glanced down at his thongs, at his mittened feet, dapper tonight in thin black socks embossed with hexagons. "What should I do? Should I leave?" she asked.

"Oh, no, Robin. Stay, unless you mind."

"The phone's over there, beside the refrigerator." She smiled. "I guess I'll go sit down."

On the sofa by the windows she pretended to read while he dialed endlessly. "Hi, this is Peter. . . . Hello, Richard? Peter. . . . Peggy, it's Peter. I said I'd call. . . ." And he was a man of his word. How many people he knew whose numbers Robin would find on her next month's bill! She eavesdropped until she wearied of so much good nature. She peeked at him, seated now on her dining table for a long call. Legs crossed, he kept time to his talk by shaking his feet. Those stockinged feet gave him an air of being housebound. Where could he go in thongs and socks? Not far, certainly. Though this evening the invalid had dressed— in sporty trousers and a plaid shirt—his feet reminded that tomorrow he'd be back in bed. And yet how brave he was, as he struck his heels against his innersoles and made a sound like running to console himself because he could not run. How uncomplaining, pale, beautiful, and nearly dead. The languishing prince! Hail!

She knew he had been hailed. She knew by the

ease with which he guffawed now, pounded her table, and said, "He bit the dust, I don't believe it, who was the girl? Naw! Her?"

He was blessed, whatever he might do, and she had come to life as an immigrant, large-nosed, far-fetched, straight from the hold. If she'd been dealt her features fairly, she'd have thrown them back, forfeited a turn, and hoped for better luck next time. As it was, she remained one of the less fortunate, envious of him, and yet admiring.

He was quiet now. She watched him stand. The table shuddered. He stretched one arm toward the wall and hung up the phone. "Thanks, Robin, but it's getting late. I've got to go." Grinning, he headed toward the door and almost sneaked off.

"Wait." She lowered her book and stared at him unobstructed. "Are you sure you're done?"

"Yes, unless . . . ." With one funny foot he held the door ajar. "Do you want something? It's not midnight yet. There's the corner store."

"Don't do me any favors. I'll send a bill."

"Oh, right." Nearly caught, he pretended to come forth voluntarily. "Some of those were toll calls. . . ."

"By the way and thanks for nothing. See you, Peter."

"What?"

"Just good night."

"Good night then."

She might as well have turned to him in profile and stuck out her tongue: look at how awful I am. Oh, let him think what he wanted, which probably was nothing, she realized. Days later, inside on a rainy afternoon, she watched him run through all the puddles in the parking lot. He wore galoshes. He carried a sodden grocery bag. He chose the farther set of stairs and bounded up. With his head in a hood, he hurried by. She heard his bolt click, his door whine open. She half-expected some sort of greeting next: "Look at you, you're soaking wet. Off with your clothes and into this bath." But no, her neighbor lived alone.

She neared their common wall as if it beckoned;
she tilted her head. Diminishing creaks. The plaintive to and fro
of metal cupboard doors. A pot lid dropped. Clatter in the kitchen.
Silence in the pipes. His bathtub dry.

But would he need baths, really? She imagined
his sweat would smell of pennies, damp, like the ones he'd held
out. *Do you have a dime?* What would he smell on her? Onions?
Fish? The back of a shop? Her shop. He'd open the door and
rattle the tin bell dangling from the transom on a piece of string.
At first he wouldn't see her, then he would, wiping her hands
across her apron bib. "What do you want?" "May I use your . . . ."
"No. Ours is a business phone. The pay booth's up the street."
On his way out, past the barrel in the aisle, she would falsely accuse
him of theft. "Put that back." She'd grab him by the arm and pry
his fist, finger by finger, until his pennies scattered on the worn
linoleum. He would leave without bothering to stoop for them.

She turned and pressed her forehead to the wall.
Not quite in the corner, she stood like that for a long while, as
though she'd found a bearing for her head, which she rolled now
and then in order to look out the window briefly.

The rain storm ended. She heard him, in his box,
move closer to hers. Then, three creaks in place, hesitation,
impatience, a stationary shuffle: all together signalling departure
soon. As a way of getting ready, he seemed to wait for someone.
Hurry up. What's keeping you? His door opened. He stepped
out. His door shut. She watched him trot past as purposeful as
a dog. Could he really have somewhere to go? something to do?
His footsteps stopped. He knocked. "Robin? May I use your
phone?"

In the weeks that followed, he visited often, always
bringing with him his small leather telephone book. Once, when
Robin glimpsed a gray-lined page, she was shocked to see addresses
noted too. Had he filled that blank as a matter of form, or did he
actually write letters sometimes? He sent birthday cards, he said.
He was a true friend. He still had friends from the second grade.

She imagined he'd been loyal all his life, and beneficent. At two years or three, he'd probably leaned forward in his stroller to offer strangers cookies, gnawed around the edges and damp with drool. "How darling. His name is Peter? No, thank you, Peter. You eat that. That's yours." He'd laugh and shake his head and take another nibble. What were cookies to him? He could always get more from his mother, or kindly bakery clerks. "Would the little boy like a cookie? Yes? Chocolate chip?" He risked nothing, while his reputation for being generous grew.

And so he said to Robin now, "I wish I could do you a favor." He had just finished dialing, and for a moment he held the receiver aloft. Then his call went through. A thin male voice cried out, "Hello? Hello? Who's there?" Peter placated it: "Doug? Peter. Hold on a second, would you?" He turned back to Robin, who was thrilled a friend of his had to wait for her. She felt contemptuous and special, until she remembered she was paying for the call. Why hadn't she gotten up the nerve to bill Peter yet? "Anything in my apartment," Peter went on, "borrow anything, Robin, long-term. Put a lien on it." He laughed. "Though I have to admit there's nothing much there."

She laughed back. "Your call," she reminded, "your friend." She walked away to her bookcase and selected another volume to hold.

She still could not read with him there. If at first she had chosen to eavesdrop, she had no choice now. She was enthralled. Each time he knocked, she felt as though she gobbled a bowl of sugar fast before answering the door. "Peter! It's you! Hello! Come in!"

She took an aspirin soon after he arrived, and between his calls she served tea. Over teacups, they discovered they were the same age ("Twenty-six, too!") and had gone to college in neighboring states. She grew up in the East, he in the West, and neither cared about his or her current job very much. After graduation, he had lived in Europe for a year. "Peter! Is that true? You're a man of the world!"

But was Peter a man of the world? No. More likely he was a large version of the child a mother might drag anywhere. *Nope. No problems with Peter. He's so well-behaved.* Nothing affected him really, not even indulgence. All that money Robin had spent treating him to phone calls? Wasted. She should have saved it for her first European tour.

"Robin, is something the matter?"

"Hmm? No." She looked up. And she saw again that he was beautiful and she was all wrong. He was good: that was it. She was back at the sugar bowl again, between spoonfuls thinking how good he was. "Do you know I'm corrupt?" she said.

"You? You're the most corrupt woman I've met."

"I'm serious. You're too good to understand."

"What?"

"That's right." If he ever discovered her thoughts, her deceptions, her motives. Calculations were tricks with sums to him. "Peter, you might find this insulting, but I have a crush on you."

"Robin, I have a crush on you."

"Yes?"

"We'll have to do something, won't we?" Across her kitchen table, he stared out, not exactly at her. She felt as if she'd handed him a dollar, and he was dazzled by a vision of the candy he might buy. "It would be a shame not to, still I want to think about it," he said. Sugar babies, honey bits, peppermint sticks, malted milk balls. In suspense, permutations could be worked out. "Let's surprise each other some time." He meant, let me surprise you. He was a hoarder and might save his dollar for weeks, but she would have him run now to the store.

"Would you kiss me?" she said.

"Sure."

They pushed from the table, met near the sink, embraced, bent down, and scrambled all over the floor on their knees together, kissing, laughing. Then they got up to take off their clothes.

Peter stepped back to look at her. "Around, around." He stirred his finger through the air. "Whirl."

She turned. "Am I all right?"

"All right? You're lovely."

"Then both of us are."

Love-ly, love-ly. What a lovely lie. She would believe it. In truth, they were clumsy together, and the only lovely things were his sounds, let out now at last, low and lovely.

Afterwards she hoped they might lie still for a minute. But no, immediately he lifted his head and asked, "Do you want to hear a joke?" She said, "Yes," and thought, he must ruin our closeness because it frightens him. But she also thought she brought them even closer because she understood. Then again, by now he might feel absolutely nothing. She heard his joke and laughed at the rapture she had found in that deluded moment before he reared his head. He was an oaf. On the chair she saw his yellow chamois chaparral shirt, reminscent of a dust cloth; on the floor his scattered footwear, thongs and socks. She wanted him to dress, be gone. But then he spoke to her. With his hands he turned her head. "Here, Robin, here, here."

He left before she fell asleep. Listening from her bed, following his progress, she pretended he was merely walking to another room, not to a separate apartment.

They always slept separately. Twice a week or three times, after finishing his calls, he undressed and stayed another hour. Or else he said, "Come to my place for a while." At best, Robin decided, he was simply pleasurable. And he was very polite to her. Say, 'Pass the sugar, please,' and do not grab, Peter.

Even she, the immigrant, knew a little etiquette. Requesting a whole night from him would be unmannerly. Besides, she only pretended to want it. Without pretense, she had no pleasure. But Peter was easy to love. He would kiss and kiss, then not kiss and with force not let her, until not kissing was better than kissing some nights. She told him, "You're tough." He hid his face in a pillow and said, "You embarrass me." He used his imagination, put it away, and in a moment was himself again, while for weeks she half believed she loved him, though she knew better.

She listened: she waited. She could not be at home without waiting for him. Was he out? Was he in? Would he knock soon? For him, their affair just made them better friends.

"It's not passionate, is it?" he asked.

"No." She was kneeling on the floor and gathering her clothes. "Have you ever had a passionate one?"

"Last summer, and then I hated her. But you and I, we're friends. Yes?"

As part of their secret, only he and she shared his slights. They had no company, though Robin imagined some: a party with Peter seated at its center, smiling, drinking, garrulous. Across the room, conscious of the air she displaced, Robin perched on a window sill. In her hand a nearly full beverage glass warmed and sweated. Even in daydreams she never outgrew herself; her time to acquire grace had passed.

She gave thanks that Peter noticed her at all. And to think that in the dark, after something arduous, he spoke just to her! "Water, water, quick, we're dying of thirst. Bring water."

He was playful. He made up rules: they must undress each other. When she reached down her leg for her sock, he said, "No help allowed. Let me." What fun, she should have liked this, but she wanted them quickly to undress themselves and then go slowly. For him, sometimes being naked was enough. When he pushed too soon, she couldn't say, "Please wait." Instead, embarrassed, furious, she made room. Part of herself got up and watched a man and a woman on the bed.

But if pleasure was the point, she must come back; she must feel herself beneath him. His smile blew out breath across her face, and she wondered what technique of hers was laughable. In the dark his small, good features vanished on a plain with holes for eyes, mouth, nostrils. His brows were fine sketches of brows, and his hair, cut to look neatly ruffled, looked no more than neatly ruffled. Across his hairless chest he was so white. White boy, she named him secretly, though his skin was no whiter than that of any other man she'd known. White boy, whitest. When he became a man he would grow hair, but now he was still a boy, above her with a man's shoulders. Even a boy could make her lose herself. The hardship came in parting from him. "Robin, it's about that time. I'm really tired." "Yes, of course. Good night." At the door she turned to look at him, lying contained within his white, white self.

He was not simple. He was more than she knew. When she rubbed her back raw by rolling with him on the carpet, he joked about "rug burn." But after the sore scabbed, he declared it "ugly" convincingly. With what ease he found the right word. How long, she wondered, had he held it ready?

Despite herself, she asked him once, "Do you like the way I look?"

"You're lovely. I told you. And exotic."

"Exotic?"

"You know, like something strange to eat."

While she drank milk from a beautiful glass, he went to the bad part of town for an ethnic meal. *The food's great, but don't inspect the kitchen, and don't use the bathroom, whatever you do.* She was sure that in a matter of time she would repulse him, utterly.

When he told her he lost his virginity on a train, she asked, "Where, in the toilet?" and startled both of them with her ignorance of sleepers riding moonlit rails. She spoke too soon, too loud, and her imagination faltered. With a rank air she revealed herself, as though a door had swung open.

"And your first time?" he asked.

"On a bed. In the background I heard radio music. While in your berth you heard the locomotive." Beside him, she lay very still and added, "How romantic."

"I didn't know what I was doing."

"Neither did I. I pretended."

"Did you fool him?"

"Probably not."

"You didn't know him well?"

"We were classmates. It was nothing, really."

"I don't mean to pry, you don't have to tell me, but altogether how many?"

So, the flower had been picked and now the leaves: defoliation. "Of course I'll tell you. Let me think." Plus one, plus one, plus one . . . . She liked to count them off while she walked sometimes; she liked to step on each of them. "Fewer than all my fingers and toes. Enough for a team."

He laughed at this.

"Now you," she said.

"Hmm . . . ."

She turned toward the wall and felt desolate for three minutes. "Well?"

"So far twenty-nine."

"So far? You haven't come to me yet?"

"You were first. From you I worked back."

Aging, she had gone the opposite route, while he grew younger. "And you're still not sure who thirty is?"

"I just unearthed her. My first year in college. True love! I remember . . . ."

Everything but her name, though he remembered other names. He had loved in sets: sisters, roommates, friends. In love, he'd corresponded, and he'd saved every envelope and letter. *Dear Peter, with all my kisses.* Love in an attic, a borrowed car, a dormitory room, an unheated cabin. All she thought love would be until she knew better, or did she? She knew he didn't love her.

"Robin, you okay? I hope I haven't said something. . . ."

"Of course not. I'm just surprised to hear you're so romantic. Actually, I suspected all along." She laughed. Ugly now, or still exotic? No matter. He was in France again with a woman named Ruth. He couldn't get enough of her. "Was she exotic?"

"Who, Ruth? No, silly, you're exotic. You."

He fluffed her hair, no longer hair but rainbow plumage. He wasn't kissing, but sampling. How exotic. How peculiar. Occasionally, a taste might develop further, into distaste. *You ate it last week, Peter. I don't understand. All right, all right. If you don't like it, leave it on your plate.*

Similarly, when he decided he did not like where he was living, he moved. "I knew from the start this was temporary, or else I couldn't have stood it. My new place is in the woods. A guest house, rent-free in exchange for doing a little carpentry work in a mansion nearby."

"So you're the kind of person who gets those kinds of deals. I always wondered."

"Now Robin."

"Now nothing."

"We'll see each other."

He spoke with such certainty that she knew he meant the opposite. "Yes," she said, "we'll see each other."

She stared at his eyes. In a certain light, the outer corners showed their wrinkles: the stamp of a citrus fruit sliced open, radiating lines. Had he suffered? No, he had squinted: through his childhood he'd played outdoors every day in a hot, sunny climate. Now he slid sunglasses from his shirt pocket, unfolded them, and put them on.

Sadness, loneliness, pain. The few times he invoked those words he seemed to be drilling for tomorrow's vocabulary quiz. *Of course you'll feel uncomfortable with these new words, Peter, but you must try to use them just the same.* Rightfully, they did not belong to Robin either.

Her problems? No more serious than her landlord's. Now that Peter was gone, perhaps she should hang a sign around her neck: Vacancy. For Rent.

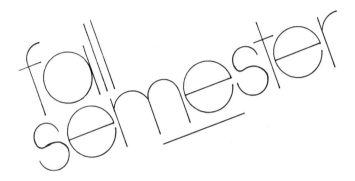

fall semester

We met in psychology lecture hall. I was crying. That was the year I was always crying. After class he took me for coffee and thick, dripping sandwiches.

"I'm unhappy," I told him.

He laughed at me.

"I want to leave school."

He howled.

"I often think about killing myself."

He fell out of the booth in hysterics.

The next day we both packed and left in his car for Long Island. In a New Jersey motel room, just minutes from the highway, we drank canned sodas with our clothes off. The shiny, quilted bedcovers rustled beneath us, and a funny, familiar odor rose. "What?" I asked him.
"Urine," he said.
"No."
"Yes. Think of the subway."
I thought of the subway. It smelled like the subway.
"We're on the platform," he said. He kissed my breasts and held them carefully. "Is the train coming?"
We checked out by three-thirty. I helped with the driving on the parkway, and we made only one other stop, at a gas station in Queens around dinner time. In the stall behind the tiled station, clutching a greasy key chain tagged "Ladies," I swayed from the scent of green disinfectant. For a moment I burst inside. I fell against the battered sink and laughed.
"Guess what happened," I said to him. We speeded down an entrance ramp onto the expressway.
"What?"
"Conception."
"What?"
"I'm pregnant. It happened in that bathroom."
"What bathroom?"
"That Esso bathroom."
"You're kidding, in that bathroom?"
In Roslyn, his mother opened the door with folded towels in her arms. "Sandor! What a surprise! And you've brought a friend with you."
"This is Karen, Mother."
"Hello, Karen. I'm on my way to Portugal. Just doing some laundry before takeoff. There are salads in the fridge if you're hungry. You look tired, Karen. Make yourself comfortable." She smiled before walking away into a linen closet.

Moving from room to room, she shouted to us while we sat at the massive kitchen table eating tomatoes and string beans. A toilet flushed. "School vacation already, Sandy?" she asked.

"No," Sandy said. "But we're taking one."

"How lucky for you." A drawer slammed. "I myself really need this trip to Portugal. Oh, Sandy, help me close my suitcase, dear."

Outside a car horn honked, and she rushed into the kitchen in a travelling suit and kissed me. "Nice meeting you, Karen. Sandy, my bags? And then come out and say hello to the Hirschmans, San. They're dropping me at the airport." She began smoothing on her other glove. "Goodby again," she said to me. "And please, see a doctor. Take care of yourself."

After she left, Sandy and I toured the house. ". . . and this is my mother's hideaway." We stood in a dark bedroom jammed full of scrolled wood furniture. "Should we sleep here?"

"I don't know. Did you tell her about me?" I picked several tennis socks and two disheveled wiglets off her bedspread. "Because she mentioned it. She told me to see a doctor."

"I didn't tell her anything."

"Maybe it shows."

"Shows? Nothing shows."

We sat on the edge of the purple bed, and as we kissed the doorbell rang.

"We better get it," Sandy said.

A tiny gypsy woman stood on the front porch. "Hello, Sandor. Remember me? I'm Elaine, your late father's distant cousin. This is my husband, Hal." She motioned toward a slumped man in striped clothing carrying a gym bag. He waved. "Is your mother home?" Elaine asked.

"No."

"Where is she?"

"She went to Portugal."

"To Portugal!"

In the kitchen we sat at the oak table again and snacked on a chocolate cake that Hal brought out of his gym bag.

"I baked it," Elaine said. "I wanted Sandy's mother to have a piece."

"You could freeze some," I suggested.

Elaine raised her brows. "Planning ahead? She's your wife, Sandor?"

"No, this is Karen, a classmate," Sandy said.

"A classmate?" Hal said.

They stayed until midnight. "By the way, I work in domestics at Alexander's in Levittown, so if you need anything," Elaine offered. "Tea towels? Carriage blankets? Crib linen?"

Hal held out her coat. "Come on, Lainie."

"No, thanks anyway. If you'll please excuse me," I said, "I have to find the bathroom."

When I unzipped my jeans in the lilac-scented powder room, I saw that my waist was gone. "My waist is gone!" I shouted.

"I think your wife is calling you, Sandor," Elaine said. "Our best to your mother, now don't forget. . . ."

The front door slammed; Sandy's soles made a clatter in the tiled hall. "Karen, are you all right?"

"No, I'm pregnant." I looked down and saw my hips widen. "But don't worry. I might be in here for a while."

Later, when I stumbled into the purple bedroom, he was wrapped in blankets and dozing. "Sandy, look what I found in the den." I clutched a creased paperback. "It's called *Nine Months of It.*"

"Hmm?"

"Page 5, 'Increased hormonal changes make frequent urination common. Also, the growing uterus nudges the bladder, which adds to the problem.' And now I have to go again. It's my first day, and I just went, and already I have to go again."

All night, hourly, I had to go again. In the morning when I moved I wanted to vomit. Then the nausea subsided, and

we showered together, noticing how my breasts had swelled.
"My God, they're heavy," Sandy said.
"Milk glands. Be gentle with them."
"And look at these." He teased my darkened nipples
and made them ache.
"What about breakfast?" I asked.
"I just want coffee."
"Coffee?"
I consulted *Nine Months of It* and drank twelve
ounces of orange juice and a quart of milk with half a loaf of
whole wheat toast, two three-minute eggs, and a cantaloupe.
I started a nutrition chart. My legs throbbed. I elevated them and
read about the second trimester while Sandy doodled in a notebook.
"I'm going to write histories," he said. "I'm going
to go out and solicit them."
"What?"
"Wasn't I a history major? I'll go through the
neighborhood writing family chronicles. I have to do something,"
he said.
"Why?"
"You can't. Just look at yourself."
My swollen legs puffed over a padded kitchen
chair. "Oh no, edema already," I moaned. My belly strained my
torn center skirt seam, and on my side a taut vee of open zipper
teeth glinted hopelessly.
"I've got to get out of here," Sandy said.
I looked up at him. "Bring back some milk, would
you?"
Exhausted, I napped all afternoon until the
doorbell rang. I wrapped myself in a loose flannel robe and
answered it.
"Hello, I'm Ira Berger from Columbia," a bearded
boy wearing tweeds said. "I came out to the Island to study matrons."
"I'm not a matron."
"But you look like a matron." He pointed a

63

mechanical pencil at me. "You're pregnant, aren't you?"

"Yes, but . . . ."

"I can see it in your face even. The pigment in your skin is darker, like you're behind a mask or something. But don't worry, it's common and goes away after pregnancy, whereas your nipples will be darker for the rest of your life."

"How did you know about my nipples?"

"I know. Also, the stripe from navel to pubic region darkens, too, and, like the change in your nipples, will be permanent. Let me part your robe and show you." He bent forward and took some flannel in his hands.

"Get away from there," I said, prying his fingers loose.

"Couldn't I ask you some more questions for a minute? Would you make me some coffee?"

"No."

He smiled. "How does your husband like you this way?"

"I'm not married. I'm not a matron. Just get out of here."

Then Sandy came up the walk with a gallon of milk in his arms. "Did you sell any histories?" I asked.

"One. To the Kleimans on Larch Street." He passed me the milk jug, and drinking straight from it, I dribbled streams down my chin.

"What histories?" Ira asked. "What do you do for a living? You're the father, right?"

Sandy turned to me. "Who is that?" he asked.

"Ira Someone from Columbia."

We stepped into the foyer, and Sandy closed the door on him.

"You sold only one history?" I asked.

"Yes."

"Oh please, I want to go back to school." I squeezed my hard, veiny breasts in my hands. "I don't want to be pregnant."

"What can we do?"

"I don't know." I started crying. When I staggered toward the stairs, I fell over a chrome magazine rack. "Sandy, help!" Fluid leaked from me, and my damp legs stuck to the scattered news weeklies. "Maybe I've miscarried." Then my stomach convulsed. "No. It's too late. I'm having labor pains."

"Karen, I'm coming," he said.

I saw him running toward me. Then the doorbell rang.

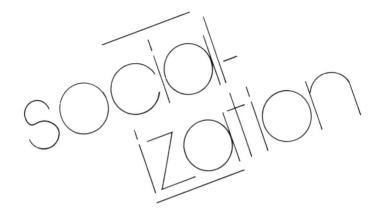

socialization

When I say I fucked my dog, I mean I fucked my dog. My parents checked out when I was a twelve-year-old. And now Zarnofsky has taken a liking to me and wants to buy me a Saint Bernard. "Too slow," I say at breakfast. "I need something friskier."

And I wonder just how much he knows. Because I don't go around telling all to all. That isn't like me.

In delicate moments I sauté onions and add tomato purée. "Sauce," I call it, and it passes. What does Zarnofsky know?

"Mitka?" he says into the telephone about a dog or a daughter or a friend somewhere. "I haven't seen her in eons. Has she been eating lately?"

He says he was married once to a ballerina, but she was actually an acrobat who gave him false expectations about the rest of us, if you understand me.

I can't come. Except with dogs, that is. Julian understood this and brought home strays. Before he left for Boston he clutched ice packs and often said, "I ache for something frozen."

Zarnofsky graphs female heat as a function of hair color. "Black is on fire," he tells me. As a medium brunette, do I severely disappoint him?

He is a historian researching American families. I only vacation. "Child rearing patterns," he calls out in his sleep. He yearns for the money to afford analysis. Currently he is writing on female socialization and the menarche. Sometimes I help him. His doctrine is feminist. Do you believe me?

Personally, I wonder how he presumes to know. "Through Freud and Marx and friends and friends of friends," he says. "Experiences relayed to me by women involved in feminist therapies. Questionnaire data and all the published material my research assistant can get her grubby hands on. And living with you and every other woman who has loved me."

If these are the bases of our new social history, I want no part of it. Please, bring me a wolfhound.

But then on my mattress, grimacing shut-eyed beneath me, he endears himself while I watch him. Hours past midnight, when street cleaners wake him, he screams for me, grasps my shoulders in his hands. "Oh, Dana," he whispers, "another headache." I bring ice water, tranquilizers, waxy earplugs. I tend the way I was meant to, and despite myself, I enjoy it.

About self-realization, career opportunities, ambition, and the slot of time which lies ahead of me: I ignore them. "Submerged and subordinated," Zarnofsky would conclude if I slipped him an anonymous case study. "I wonder when she started menstruating?" At twelve and a half, and as it is, I'm just fine for him. "The woman of the future," he laughs, curling my hair in his hands.

And everything goes to the dogs. Do you know what I'm talking about? I have never risen above that low level of the hairy and the sexual.

But who wants to listen to me? The same tedium applies for millions. The questionnaire data alone supports me. Edith R., aged 24, Patricia M., aged 30, Louisa W., aged 35, and Irene and Nona P., aged 52 and twins, all refer to themselves as failures. Perhaps I should travel the country and locate them. "Hello," I would call from their porches. "How familiar are you with the local animal pound?"

However, no time for this now. Mitka has come to visit. She is human, aged six, and Zarnofsky's daughter from a very short marriage. She creates jewelry out of interlocking plastic balls. "Poppa beads," she calls them. For a week at least, Zarnofsky has been wearing a pink and white choker.

"Mitka Zarnofsky," he announces to me in the bathroom, "has decided to become a brain surgeon."

"This morning she wanted to be a bride."

"My God, it's all so cultural. Has she been watching television?"

Most of her day she watches television. She won't enroll in school this year. "So she doesn't like it," Zarnofsky says. "Can I blame her? She's a six-year-old libertine."

She laughs out loud at herself. She cooks cheese casseroles. She fingerpaints and walks the house naked. Why do I hold these things against her?

"Because!" says Zarnofsky, smiling, pouring wine for himself. "Isn't it natural?"

"You're barking up the wrong tree," I tell him, "if you're looking for the natural."

"Oh, right. You're so different," he says. "Aren't you?"

No. In the mirror, quite ordinary, except for the hair and the eyes, with those green half-moons beneath them. In bed, nothing special either. But then, it all depends on the company. In the kitchen, adequate, sometimes a failure with leafy vegetables. Alone in a room, however, great company, though leading yourself in circles can be dizzying. You don't go very far either.

Oh, Mitka, my dear, I didn't mean to change the subject. Even when he named you, Zarnofsky had the best in mind. Why should I begrudge you your happiness, aside from the fact that we all know what misery loves?

But am I miserable? I may be ecstatic and just not know it. Distinctions blur so frequently, and the piled laundry mounts. How do you tell whose socks are whose? With underwear, it's a different story, but who wears any? Since she was trained, Mitka tells me, she hasn't stepped into a pair. And the hamper, which overflowed into the hallway on Tuesday, is still surging. Soon all three of us will be naked at the dinner table with only napkins over our laps. Should this distress me?

Mitka says no. Zarnofsky says no, too, but I ask him to pinch his paunch and reconsider. As usual, the lone dissenter, I say yes and wonder out loud what has happened to decorum.

"That question," Zarnofsky answers, "from you of all people."

Of all people, me. Of all dogs, the golden shepherd I am patting on the back. Of all places, the park where Mitka dissects daisies like a botanist and Zarnofsky, on a far bench, drafts a letter to his friend the psychohistorian.

"Dana!" Zarnofsky shouts. "What is the medical term for irregular mid-cyclical spotting?"

"Irregular mid-cyclical spotting." Sometimes life is so easy for me. And the lovely shepherd is licking my neck now.

How to slip away with him? I wonder.

But his owner, smiling with discovery from the southern tulip bed, calls out, "Corky, boy," and approaches. "Hello, boy." When he whistles and waves I recognize him as an old friend of Julian who may well know the truth about me. "Thata boy, Corky." He claps and my shepherd runs to him. Obviously his priorities are not what I'd hoped for. His name, either. But you win and you lose. The ball bounces, and in desperation, you try something different with your hair now and then.

Mitka's was long until very recently, when she pared it down with a serrated vegetable knife. "My wild child," Zarnofsky calls her now. "My little hedge head."

"I couldn't stand it," Mitka tells me. "It got in the way of things, especially fingerpainting."

And I think we are beginning to understand each other, even though my own hair, loosely ringletted, twirls past my shoulders. Zarnofsky likes it this way. "Is that sexist of me?" he asks. What can I say to him about matters of sexual preference? In an ideal world of unlimited opportunities, even I would prefer long hairs.

But I make do with what I have. A fleshy, slightly hirsute man who tries very hard and whispers, "I love you, all of you, even your nose," at the strangest moments. Like when I'm on the verge of something I have never fallen over.

Why can't I come with a man? I ponder this while doing sit ups. If I'm going to try at all, why not get the best of it, at least sometimes? Of course this line of thought is hardly a new one. In fact, it's ragged, dog-eared. Strained and nearly snapped, like almost everything.

Perhaps another lover. Perhaps a former lover. "Julian?" I print on the steamy bathroom. "Who's that?" Mitka asks. I forgot she can read already.

"A man I lived with before your daddy."

"Oh, yes. Julian. Now I remember. I've heard all about him."

"What about him?" What about me, begging for
clues from a six-year-old? However precocious, still a six-year-old.
"He wrote to you. Here's the letter."
Scrawling on torn newspaper margins, he sends
his love and asks, "How's history? Menstruation? And that man
who claims to study both of them? Has he succeeded where I failed?
For me, I hope not; for you, otherwise. When will I see you again?
Soon? Please? Julian."
"Some note," Mitka says after I fold it and stuff it
in my bra. "I love reading over shoulders. I just learned how."
"You're a barefoot sneak," I say, running after her
toward the kitchen. Then, in spite of myself, "Mitka, what do you
think of it?"
"It's your life," she answers. "But if I were you,
I would risk it."
Mitka Zarnofsky, naked truant and daughter of the
man who fucks me, advises me to risk it. I consider. Should I risk it?
"Mitka, may I fix you lunch or something? Are you
hungry?"
"Do you know how to make jelly omelets?"
I make five, and Mitka gobbles all.
"Where do you put it?" I ask her.
"I'm afraid I'm anorexic. Haven't eaten for a week,
but no one noticed," she says, wiping jelly off her chest. "I took
the platters to my room and gave them to the pigeons. On the
window sill. So now I'm force feeding."
"Oh, Mitka."
"Don't feel sorry for me. I know you do."
"But Mitka."
Why can I say nothing more than her name to this
child? How can I help her?
"Just leave me alone," she says. "I'm independent."
Wearing nothing under her hooded tweed coat,
she confers with me on a stone wall in the park. "Of course my
father doesn't understand. Why do you think my mother left him?
But I love him just the same."

"I love him, too."

"But he's not your father."

"No."

Then, I never thought he was, did I? No, I moved beyond simplistic Freudianisms years ago, didn't I? When I discovered dogs?

"Is it true about the dogs?" Mitka asks.

"I'd rather not talk about it now."

Because the Afghan near the elm tree strolls nearer and I tremble. But he passes.

"I masturbate," Mitka says. "Doesn't everyone?"

"No, not everyone."

Just what can you say about everyone that goes beyond respiration and heartbeat? Later I wash vegetables and consider this quite seriously until Zarnofsky enters the kitchen leading a woman by the hand.

"Dana, meet Lowenfeld, my new assistant. She's analyzing the questionnaire data from the high school study. This is Dana, my housemate."

"Housemate?" I shake dry a colander full of mushrooms and smile so domestically. "Are you staying for dinner, Lowenfeld?"

"Of course she is," Zarnofsky tells me.

At the table, passing mushrooms, walnuts, and cheese, Lowenfeld reveals herself. "I'm a graduate student in sociology. I've been studying the family for thirteen months now. Rethinking it, you might say. As a woman sociologist, I have a lot to contribute. I have a lot to say."

Then spit it out. Time's wasting. Look at me, for example.

But even Zarnofsky refuses to take a glance when, alone with me in our bedroom, he declares Lowenfeld the perfect role model for Mitka. "Perfect," he tells the windows.

"Then why not replace me with her?"

"In due time, why not?" He struggles with his

pajama top then pokes his head through. "Who knows how things will work out? And you'll have time to find another man to live with. Bring home anyone. I'd like to meet them all."

"Do as you please with Lowenfeld, but as far as other men are concerned, I'd rather not introduce you. Or to dogs, either."

"It's up to you, Dana."

"What about Mitka?"

"Mitka? You'll see her, I guess."

"Well, I hope so. We like each other."

"She likes everyone. She's a child."

Ah, the generosity of children. They are such wonderful loving things. I must have some of my own someday.

"You'll never have children," Zarnofsky prophesies. "It just isn't in you."

"But they're in me already," I tell him. "Mutts. Here." I flatten his hand over my belly. "Can't you feel their tails wagging?"

Under those flannel smock tops, Lowenfeld, too, may be concealing something. Around the house, she winds herself in plaid horse blankets. Oh, did I mention that she's moved in with us? Really, she's a very friendly woman. Exactly what Zarnofsky needed for himself, though I fear for Mitka.

And the whole house shudders as she stomps over books and papers, periodicals, tables, and chairs. "I won't go to school," she shouts. "I tell you, I won't."

"But Mitka, the law says you have to," Lowenfeld reasons. "And I think it would be lots of fun."

"Yes, Mitka, you're missing out on a lot at school," Zarnofsky adds. "Don't you want to make friends?"

"I'm friends with Dana."

"But Dana's going away."

"Where?"

Who knows, Mitka. Any suggestions? Julian called

to welcome me, but why go on repeating myself?

"Yes, life shouldn't be boring," all of us, including
Lowenfeld, agree at dinner.
"Bruce tells me you're leaving tomorrow," she
says. "What can I do to help?"
"Bruce?"
"Me. Bruce Zarnofsky," Zarnofsky says.
"Will you get a dog?" Mitka asks. Even in
a corduroy school dress, she is still the same child.
"I don't think so."
I can't afford it, and besides, it's not the same when
you buy.
In the morning we walk to the bus stop together.
"This is where I board for school," she says.
"I'll ride there with you."
Pressed together on the long rear seat between two
secret smokers, we huddle in a fog, whispering.
"I can't stand her," Mitka says. "But I'll get used
to it."
"She's not that bad."
"Will I see you?"
"Of course you will. Soon."
"Where are you going?"
"Not far."
But alone, with neither hound nor man. For
a while, at least. Then I'll want someone I can talk with.
"I'll miss you."
"Oh, Mitka."

docu-
mentary

One girl carved her legs with a silver art tool. Her roommate pressed her shoulder to a burning light bulb until the skin crisped. A junior upstairs grated her cheeks like cheese. And someone else tied plastic bags over her head, though always in the final moments, when the bags clung damply to her features and left no room for breath, tore them open with her fingernails. All damage was done softly, in seclusion, without audible signs of pain.

·

"HYPNOSIS AND PAIN"
A lecture by Professor H. K. Maglin of Randall University
2:30 P.M., April 19, Psychology Seminar Room 10

•

Page 17 from the sophomore year journal of Rita Schlossberg: I hate myself. Hence the need to pull my face off, bang my forehead against the edges of buildings, desks, lunch counters, and the like. The cranium collapses, the blood flows forth, the rage is satisfied, I imagine, somehow.

•

It was all the rage to be enraged. In a quiet way, it was very popular. Self-mutilation flourished all over campus.

•

Dr. Rickerson of Psychological Services: They are girls with time on their hands. They hurt themselves when they should be doing schoolwork. In a study of employed self-mutilators, the rate of mutilation was found to be highest on weekends, when the subjects had nothing better to do with themselves.

•

Mrs. Kirsty Radaway, Assistant Dean of Women, in an informal luncheon discussion: I was the Dean on Duty last weekend, and during that short period of time alone, there were two cases. On Saturday morning, a freshman was taken to the inpatient psychiatric ward at U. Hospital. Several of her hallmates had found her in her dorm room, amidst broken records and album dust jackets, crying uncontrollably. She could not say what was wrong, but she had cut her neck and arms with a razor blade and was bleeding quite profusely. On Sunday afternoon, the intern on duty summoned me to the infirmary to escort a second student to an off-campus institution. University Hospital's ninth floor was all filled up, and the young woman in question, a sophomore, was hysterical, also bleeding, and in desperate need of hospitalization. She had jabbed herself with manicure scissors. Her roommate accompanied us in the campus police van to the private facility. Once inside, as we followed a resident down a bright corridor, the roommate reassuringly said, "Susan, really, it's like a vacation. Think of this as a resort." "Yes," Susan said, "the last one."

•

Schlossberg, page 23: I want to throw myself away, down staircases, into traffic against the lights. I want to climb to the dark side of the subway tracks and die. Why?

•

Conversations overheard by a resident advisor in the Margaret Stern-Smith Class of '34 Student Lounge:
1. "Of course I'm lonely here. I've never been lonelier. For months it's been this way, but I haven't been able to tell anyone. You're the first person I've told."
2. "It's not that I can't do the work. I don't think I'm stupid. But I don't want to do the work, and I can't. I look at the pages and cry."
3. "It's a breeze if you go to see your advisor. Just bring in a psychiatric excuse, and they'll let you drop anything. They'll let you revamp your schedule in the middle of finals week."

•

Lany Binet, doctoral candidate and part-time lecturer, Department of English, at a friend's dinner party: I assigned them *Notes from Underground* last week, and some of the kids said it was too depressing. Uselessly depressing. In a way, I think that's healthy. When I was a freshman, I would have said, "Oh, yes," fervently. I was writing suicide notes all over the place in my most flowery hand. Would you believe it, that winter I tried to kill myself for the first time.

•

Excerpts from table talk, early dinner shift, Hathaway Dining Triangle:

1. "I'd rather not see my professors outside of class. I don't want to eat dinner with them, though I hear it may become mandatory."
   "You're kidding."
   "No. I have enough trouble talking to peers."
2. "When I was at the Briar School, every Friday I drove with another girl into town to buy the stuff. The two of us went because she owned a car, and with my hair up, I looked like someone much older. I wore a selection of pooled jewelry and carried a lit cigarette and always bought about forty dollars worth, mostly wine, for the whole floor. We had an established fund for it. But here it's different. I sit on my bed and drink alone.

.

Dr. Rickerson, Psychological Services: They need strictly scheduled classroom and library hours. Teachers should take attendance. More written work should be assigned. And I'm all in favor of organized social activities as well, mixers at the Union or in one of the Dining Commons, perhaps. We've got to get them out of those dorms.

.

Rita Schlossberg, initial interview, Psychological Services: This fall when my mother brought me here, she cried when she saw my room. The southern wall was crumbling, and there were plaster chips all over the bed. After I unpacked my things, we walked with some empty suitcases back to the lot where she'd parked the car. When she started crying again, I left her but then turned around and saw her wiping her eyes, standing in a vacant space next to two white bags. She calls on Sundays, but we have nothing to say.

.

Mrs. Kirsty Radaway, Assistant Dean of Women: Of course there's a tendency to blame the parents, but there comes a time when you can't blame the parents. These girls are women, and they've got to take responsibility for themselves.

•

Lany Binet, doctoral candidate and part-time lecturer, Department of English, to a friend in the dark: One time I swallowed vials, literally vials, of variously colored pills. When I woke up in the hospital, there was a telegram from my father. "Congratulations, Lany," it said. "At last you've succeeded in getting my attention."

•

Schlossberg, page 17: My father lurks behind elm trees in a poplin raincoat, his eyes shaded with deep green glasses, his umbrella in hand. "Storm threats," he whispers, laughing, vanishing and reappearing with ghostly agility.

•

Junior discovered crouched under a basin, third floor women's restroom, Van Marttel Library: Leave me alone. Get out. If my parents ask, tell them I won't move from here.

•

Schlossberg, page 3: The bathrooms are the only safe spots, but even there, locked in a stall, who knows who will find you? Where to hide when you're already so lonely?

•

Conversation, basement phone booth, Burnett Hall, noontime: No, he can't call me back. I'm at a pay phone, and I can't sit here waiting all day. I have a class now. I'm late for a class. No, my appointment's not until Thursday, but please, can't I see him sooner? Well, maybe he could give me a prescription or something. Tell him I'm dying.

•

Dr. Rickerson: If the causes were biochemical, we could prescribe and send them on their ways. But as it is, we have to talk to them. Daily, our staff of thirteen spends hours talking to them. Yes, each student is allowed ten visits, but so many need more. What can we do with them? U. Hospital Outpatient doesn't want them. Community Aid doesn't want them. And they all can't afford private care, that's certain, especially when you consider how much their parents are already paying for tuition.

•

Second session, Rita Schlossberg and Dr. Bert Fischel, Psychological Services:

Fischel: Tell me some more about your parents.

Schlossberg: I told you all there is. My mother's a fool, and my father's dead.

Fischel: And you're very angry with them this morning, aren't you, Rita?

•

Mrs. Kirsty Radaway to freshman advisee: Yes, I will grant you permission to drop the biology lab. Though I wish you'd reconsider. Why not try it for another few weeks? And you say you *have* talked with Professor Maizel? Well, how is everything else going? No, I'm sorry. You'll have to inform your father that a partial tuition refund is impossible at this point.

•

Professor Maurice Letcher, Department of English, during office hours with Rita Schlossberg:

Letcher: I admire what you did with the creative exercise, Rita. "A" work, as you see. But I'm a little worried about you. I know several excellent people at Psychological Services. I can give you their names and . . . .

Rita: I've already been assigned to someone over there.

•

Dr. Rickerson, Psychological Services: Of course there are disagreements here, but that's not unusual. A few of the younger men on the staff talk about the adolescent's need for space. I say they need structure, not space. Why give them more space when they're already lost in it?

•

Schlossberg, page 20: How to make contact with the dead? How to reach back, down, under? How to make bones talk?

•

Lany Binet, Department of English, shouting to her ten o'clock class: Close your notebooks for a minute and look at me. Sometimes I think you're all dreaming. Why don't you laugh occasionally? Can't you tell when I'm being sardonic? Laugh!

•

Conversations, Van Marttel Library, snack center, 12:30 A.M.:
1. "It's not like math, where there's a right or a wrong answer. It's all subjective. You're at the teacher's mercy, and so many of them are crazy."
2. "All the lights in this place buzz. I can't study here."
"Then go home."
"It's too late. I'll never get it done if I go now. In eight hours it's due."
3. "She's talking to herself."
"Where? Who?"
"The one in the corner."

•

Schlossberg and Fischel, fifth session:
Schlossberg: Sometimes I stay at the library very late, but then I'm terrified to go home. I'm terrified in the library, too. I hear there's a man in a snow mask who rapes women in the bathrooms.
Fischel: I haven't heard that. Do you really think it's true?
Schlossberg: Yes, it's true. Of course it's true. Don't you believe me?

•

Lany Binet, to a male colleague complaining of

depression: Go out and get drunk and get fucked. You need fucking. I'd even go with you myself if I weren't already busy.

•

Rita Schlossberg, third line, Creative Exercise, English 107, Professor Letcher: My father's in my ear, singing in my ear.

•

Mrs. Kirsty Radaway to Rita Schlossberg during the required sophomore advising session: Oh, I see you're from Albany. Is your father in government?

•

Dr. Rickerson: It's a shame, I admit it, but because of limited filing space, we destroy all psychiatric records after ten visits or three months, whichever comes first, though we do know which students have visited us and which haven't yet. It might be interesting to go back over the records, if they were available, in ten years or so and do a generational study, but really, I see five students a day, three quarters of them female, and it all boils down to the same thing: sex.

•

Fischel and Schlossberg, session six:
Fischel: You haven't mentioned sexuality.
Schlossberg: Sexuality.
Fischel: What about it?
Schlossberg: I was promiscuous when I first got here. Everyone on my floor was. But it wore off.

•

Lany Binet to another colleague at the faculty club: Twice a week for five years I went. I couldn't stop talking, then one day I shut up. Eventually everyone goes and eventually everyone stops. What can I say? You grow up.

•

Schlossberg, page 36: I know a tree is a tree,

a desk lamp is a desk lamp, but everything is so bright my eyes
ache. Unbearable clarity. Why am I always shaking?

•

During an accidental meeting at the campus drug
store, Professor Maurice Letcher to Rita Schlossberg, who runs
away without answering: Rita, I haven't seen you in a while.
You're still taking my class, aren't you?

•

Dr. Rickerson: It saddens me both professionally
and personally to say this, but there are some students we'll never
begin to help. It took them eighteen, nineteen, twenty years to get
this way. How can we change them overnight?

•

Schlossberg, page 42: I want to scream. I want to
sever limbs and throw them out windows. I want to shoot to kill
and never miss target. God (a figure a speech), help me. My
God, someone help me.

•

Lany Binet, laughing in a bar: Well, in every
population there are crazies.

•

Dr. Bert Fischel to Rita Schlossberg, tenth session:
I wonder if you know what you mean some of the time. Like when
you say you're not happy. What do you mean by "happy"? Isn't it
something pretty superficial you're after? When you leave here
today, Rita, take a look at the world and ask yourself who's happy.

•

Schlossberg, page 47: Happy? Oh yes, thank
you. So happy.

The woman in the photograph (page 235)
cups a hand to her neck. Her pale hair
waves past high cheekbones as she
peers out at something, someone, beyond the right-hand page. Is
it you?

I crack the book in half and go on bending it. You
rustle in bed. I hear the springs moan, then your feet on the
floorboards. "Lunch," you shout, as if that's my name.

"Grilled cheese," I answer. "I smell it burning."

We live in a motel room with closeted kitchen

facilities. We have free parking, but nothing to park. A weedy garden deck surrounds the drained swimming pool, and in the palm tree, rats nest.

"Damn it!" A cheese bubble scalds your mouth.

"Be careful," I warn. "It's hot."

Naked, you stand over the sink, your hand held as your plate, at chin level. Strings of cheese stretch from your lips, and you jerk your head back to tug at them. Your eyes change. You've noticed something. "The book. My anthology. What are you doing with it?"

"Nothing. I was reading it."

"What about the binding?"

"Intact." Camouflaging the worst of it with my hand, I hold it up and flip to the well-worn page. "Here's Cedar." I flash her photograph. "Still looking for you."

"Don't joke about her."

"Cedar Fisher," I read aloud, "born on July 14, 1950. She was married once, but now has settled alone on a wooded stretch in northern California. She is a voice teacher as well as a poet. Her books of verse include *Mirrors* and *Cone,* both published by Tidal Press. Sometimes she gives local readings. 'For years,' she says, 'I have been digging for love.'"

"Shut up."

"But those are the facts about her. Public knowledge, don't you agree?"

You ignore me and reheat the early morning coffee. You brush crumbs from your hands onto your legs, so much hairier than the rest of you that they look like leggings. You find a scab, pick at it.

"It's easy to see," you announce, "why you envy her."

•

In her piney cabin, sparsely furnished in squared, blonde hardwood, a honey jar catches light on the kitchen tabletop. Leafy cuttings root in clear jelly glasses. A poem you wrote for

her is framed on the eastern wall. From every window, a view
of . . . . What? Evergreens?
"Give me her letter again," I say. "The one with
descriptions."
"Leave me alone."
"I want to check something."
"Just shut up. I'd be with her already if I had a car."
Instead you lie in this room with me, the Jew you
mistakenly married on a dark-haired day. Sitting on the floor in
a linted black cardigan, I scan the puzzle features in last week's
newspapers. I grip a pencil between my teeth. In our bed, you
read a volume of her poetry and brood.

     .

     At supper you reject what I've cooked for you,
something curried out of cottage cheese and peas.
"It's good," I tell you. "And I made it in a closet,
which makes it even more wonderful."
"Go to hell," you say, but I refuse to.

     .

     Outside by the pool, I watch for rats, a glimpse of
tail or ear, something moving through the weeds with whiskers.
The patch of tall spiked grass by my lawn chair looks flattened, as
if a neighbor has fallen into it. Beyond it, in the pool, gray and
green birds hop back and forth over the crack near the diving
area. I skim through a dated magazine.
     Then a Saab pulls up, parks by the charcoal grill.
Muttering to herself, her shawled back to me, she slides out,
reaches over the front seat for something. A basket. Her long
hair looks tangled, thinner than in her photograph. It needs
washing. She wipes it from her eyes. She cups her fingers to her
neck. She sighs.
"Cedar. Over here."
"David?" She calls your name. "Is that your wife
with you?"
"He's inside. I'm alone."

"Oh, hello." She waves an arm like a branch. "Could you help me carry some things?"

I take the grocery bags. "I packed enough for a few meals," she says. "In his letters David complained so bitterly of the food here."

"Did you tell him to cook it himself?"

"I don't think he likes to." Her wooden shoes clap over the parking lot. As she swings her basket, her shawl unwinds, falls to her side, and drags. "Would you get that for me? I think I might trip over it. Oh, I'm sorry. I've forgotten your name."

"Joan. And I can't. My hands are full. Besides, we're here already." I stop at our door and kick it open.

You, sprawled naked in bed, your back to us, throw a flowered bath towel over yourself. "I'm cold. Close the door. Close the door, Joan." You glance down at a page of something. My cookbook? "Goddamn it, close the door."

"Are you hungry?" I ask.

"I didn't eat dinner."

"'Whose fault was that?"

"Listen . . . ." You roll over, your wrinkled towel sliding to your thighs. "Cedar." You see her. "My God."

"David." She sets her lidded basket down. "I was so worried from your letters . . . ."

"Cedar, I can't believe this."

She steps out of her clogs toward you. "How I've missed you," she says, laughing, bending over at the bedside, taking your penis in her fist first, before sucking it.

"Cedar," you repeat. "My God."

·

On the pool deck, lit dimly by the soda machine, I open a can of root beer and drink. Later I climb down the pool ladder and lie in a corner of the deep end. When I touch the pool walls with my fingertips, a damp dustiness that smells like moss rubs onto them. Fungus.

"Joan?" She's followed me. "Are you out here?"

"I'm in the pool."

"The pool?" she asks. Then I see her in a winged kimono, squatting above me, closer to the shallow end. "I *thought* this pool was dry." She pats a sack next to her. "I came out to use the ice machine, but I wanted to talk to you, too. About what happened. When I saw him I couldn't help myself. I'm like that sometimes." She laughs. "I'm so spirited."

"What do you need ice for?"

"Oh. We're taking a bath in it."

"Why?"

"It's exciting. But Joan, really, I wish you wouldn't avoid the issue. We all must sit down and talk about it."

"You'd better clean out the tub first."

"What?"

"We never clean it out. It's filthy." I stand up suddenly and dizzied, boost myself out of the pool. "Are you ready to go back now?"

·

"I didn't lock it," she says as she taps our dented door open. "David?"

"In the bathroom," you say.

"I have the ice. I'm a piece of ice," she shouts, running to you.

"Joan's back?" Still naked, you lean out of the bathroom doorway and spot me.

"I think she's an ass," I say. "She's worse than her photograph."

·

"Cedar?" The word shakes when you say it. "What's taking so long?" You crouch in the tub on ice piled beneath you like rock candy. "Cedar?"

"She wants to freeze you," I say from the bath mat. "Then haul you back north with her."

"David, I'm in the kitchen," she says. "Making tea."

"What about this bath?"

"Oh, let's forget it. I'm so tired."

"She's making a fool of you," I say when you lurch out of the tub, the ice avalanching. "Get rid of her." I hand our yellow towel to you then rub your numbed legs awake with the green one.

"Let her finish her visit."

"No. She may never leave."

"Then leave yourself."

"I don't want to. Remember, I live here."

"So do I." You take my head in your chilled hands, shove it back against the light switch.

.

"When I first met David in college, he was so fickle," Cedar says. "Mainly during our senior year. Are you sure you don't want tea, Joan?" She lifts the ceramic pot she brought with her. "It's herbal. Won't keep you awake."

"I don't want any."

"Well," she continues, "the week we met he told me he loved me in a movie theater." She fits her teacup in her saucer and frowns. "But then we broke up and after graduation, drifted apart, writing letters every once in a while, sometimes trading poetry. Of course, I went through a disastrous marriage and a divorce the following year, and when David told me this past October that *he* had married, I couldn't believe it."

"It was sudden," you say.

"How did you meet?" she asks. "Tell me. I'd like to write about it."

.

During the night, whispers from the floor wake me. I reach for your pillow and feel only damp mattress.

"Why her?" she asks. "What in the world did you see in her?"

"Shh. She can hear you."

"No, she's sleeping."

"I don't know. I thought she was funny. Cedar,
I told you. It was a mistake."
"Then why don't you leave her. What are you
doing here?"
"We couldn't afford it anywhere else. We had
some money after we sold her car. So we thought we'd stay here to
decide."
"Decide what?"
"What to do next."
"Did you decide?"
"No."
"So leave her. Come north with me. Maybe you
would start to write again."
Then weight shifts, the boards bend, and low
groans shoot across the room to me. I cover my ears.

·

In the morning she fries eggs. "How would you
like yours?" she asks.
"I don't eat eggs. Where's David?"
"I sent him out. So I could talk to you. Bacon?"
"What do you want?"
"I've spoken to David, and he thinks he might write
verse again." She slaps her spatula down. "Wouldn't that be
wonderful?"
"Not unless he's better at it."
"Oh, Joan. You're so negative. You remind me of
a poem I wrote, called, 'The Way That Life Moves.' It's part of my
personal mythology. Would you like to hear it?"
"No."
"What do you plan to do with yourself, Joan?"
"You want David, don't you?"
"Well, I'd . . . ."
"Then trade me your car for him."
"What?"

"The Saab. Give me the Saab."

"That car cost ten thousand dollars. And I just finished the payments on it."

"Good."

"It's ridiculous, Joan. Mercenary," she says, tugging at the neck of her leotard, twisting her string of shells. "No. Mercenary. I refuse."

.

You say, "I hear you want Cedar's car."

"To make up for the other one," I tell you. "The one you sold."

"Oh," Cedar says from the window. "Let's talk about children. I just saw two outside. They're so wonderful. Would you like some?"

"Yes." You tilt your head slightly.

"We could teach them things," she tells you. "In the pine forests."

.

When it's dark, she remembers dinner. "We haven't eaten yet. And I wanted to make soufflé with zucchini." She holds up three like fingers. "But we're out of cream. Would you go get some, Joan?"

"Don't trust her with the car," you say.

"No, David," Cedar answers. "This is to show her that I do trust her with the car."

.

Barefoot, avoiding broken glass, she wades across the parking lot with me. At the car, she unlocks the driver's door, drops the keys in my palm.

"No, the deal's off. You can't have him," I say. I toss the keys back. She catches them.

.

In the room she stuffs her kimono in her basket,

then wraps her teapot in her shawl. "Your wife won't leave you," she says, laughing.

      You tug a pair of pants on.

      "She absolutely refused to, David."

      To me, she says, "You blew it, Joan. And we're going north to write poetry."

      Your striped blue shirt trails from the closet doorknob. You reach for it, slip it on, and leave with it open, like a jacket.

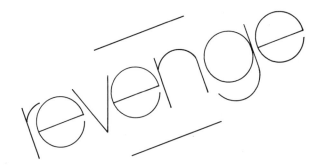

revenge

We don't know why she disappeared or why she mailed back Mother's checks before she walked off to who knows where, or perhaps someone drove her. She doesn't have a car herself, and the police say she sold her bicycle. Anyone in her right mind would have cashed those checks before vanishing. "I can't accept these checks," she wrote. "But I want you to know that I greatly appreciate everything. I have decided to change my name and default on my education loans. Don't try to look for me." She has always tended toward melodrama. When she was thirteen she strode bleary-eyed into a drugstore to buy a bottle of aspirin to kill herself with. She thought you could kill yourself with aspirin. Once inside, distracted by the magazine rack on the main aisle, she forgot about pain killers and wasted her dollar on something called "Teen" or "Sixteen" or "Fifteen." You know the kind of periodical: the numerically descriptive name always appeals to a younger set, the audience toward whom it's aimed anyway.

"I don't buy magazines now," she said the last time she visited. We were standing in a grocery, in line at the checkout. "I look at them while waiting in places like this." Casually, she chose that week's "Notorious" from a stack near the chewing gum. "Or else I go to the library. You'd be surprised at all the junk they have in the library."

No, her terrible tastes haven't changed, but that day even she mocked them. "You have to laugh at yourself," she said later, tossing a throw pillow in my living room.

"Put that pillow down," I told her. It was one of many I've needlepointed. But she doesn't approve of crafts. She doesn't approve of needlepoint.

"Look." She prodded my block initials, stitched in red at the tip of a bargelloed conch shell. "It's like signing your name to follow-the-dots. Why don't you stop buying kits and make up your own patterns?"

"I don't have to defend myself to you. So you've read more books than I have. Does that make you a better secretary?" After eighteen years in the classroom, she types for a living. "And it's not even a living. Mother told me about the checks she sends you. In California." Paradise burst with a needlepoint. See, I can be as clever as she thinks she is. "I know what you really are. At twenty-five, an aging, depressed camper in black tee shirt and khakis, riding a bicycle." I smiled. That always has bothered her.

"Witch," she said. "Everyone knows you're uglier."

"Would you like my magnifying mirror? I have

one that will triple the size of your laugh lines. Before you know it, you'll have a definite muzzle. You should take better care of your skin. If only you weren't still battling acne."

"You . . . ."

She wanted to hit me, I could tell. I decided to let her pound me like a pillow for old times' sake. Then I would strike once, hard, and make her crumple before telling Mother, who was visiting, too, and dozing in the family room. But over the years, my sister has learned to sublimate. Instead of me, she turned on my seashell puff, which is backed with velveteen, and bit into a corner of it. She gritted. She wrenched. But the piping defeated her.

"Do your gums ache?" I took the pillow, damp with saliva and dashed with teeth marks, away from her. "You're worse than a dog. Why don't you rest your head in your paws? Go lie down somewhere."

I left her crying in the dining room, Mother still asleep on one of the downstairs loungers. "See you later," I called. It was two-thirty, time to pick up Stefan, my son, at his nursery school.

When I came back with Steffy, who was plucking at a necklace he'd strung that afternoon, I found both Mother and Anna slouched on the family room sofa and glaring at the fish tank. "Hello," I said from the top of the stairs. "The life's gone out of Anna, I see. Mother, you're awake again."

Steffy scrambled down the steps, one at a time but quickly, and shouted, "Hi, everybody."

"Hi," Anna said, turning away her face, sallower than ever above her favorite dreary crew neck.

Stefan rushed to Mother and tugged at the knitting in her lap. Mother said, "Oh, I forgot I was working on this. Betsy, I know you two were fighting. Make up."

I shook my head. "I don't want to aggravate you with the details, Mother."

"Aggravate," Stefan murmured.

"I'm sorry." Anna barely moved her lips. "I'm oh so."

"I'll bet you are." I smiled. "Zombie."

"Stop it," Mother said. "When you two fight, it's a knife in my side."

"And Betsy twists it," Anna said.

"Who dug it in in the first place?" I asked. "Who carries a bowie in her pants pocket?"

"Stop it! Stop it! If you don't, I'll bang your heads together." Instead, Mother gripped Stefan's head, he cried, and then she hugged him. "See how you confuse me?"

"It's a game, Steffy," I said. He nestled his face in Mother's bosom and giggled there. "That's right, make nice. Nana's sorry. Aren't we all."

"Yes," Anna sobbed, "that I'm alive."

"Well." I hesitated. "Only most of the time."

"You girls take my heart and tear it. *I* could die." Mother dropped her cheek onto Anna's black cotton shoulder and wept out loud. "My own flesh and blood. Both."

Startled, Stefan lifted his head with a wail.

"Mommy's coming, Steff." I stumbled downstairs and onto the sofa with tears in my own eyes.

"Girls," Mother said.

"Betsy," Anna said.

"Anna," I said.

Mother clutched my neck, Stefan, sighing, curled on my hip, wiped his nose with a hank of my hair, and I stretched some fingers to my sister, who squeezed them hard. For five minutes at least, we hugged and whispered ("I'm sorry," "No, *I'm* sorry," "Forgive me," "Why do we?" and "Never again") while Stefan parroted us and hummed. That's how we settle things in our family, although nothing stays settled for long.

But happiness hovered for a while. Uncharacteristically generous, Anna began cooking dinner, manicotti from scratch, dough, filling, and sauce. She puttered in the kitchen until six. (Quite therapeutic. That's why I encouraged her, even though my husband, Solomon, is not a pasta eater.) Only one crisis arose. Unobserved, Stefan patted his baby hands in the bowl of grated Parmesan, licked his fingers and patted again, scratched his scalp, picked his nose, and wiped his hands on his jersey and jodhpurs (in whatever order). When the bowl overturned, we finally discovered him, fuzzy all over with pale cheese dust. "No," Anna said, "oh no."

"Don't worry, he's fine. Mother," I called, my palm raised to keep my laughing son at arm's length, "would you wash Steff?"

Squirming, he whined, "Leave me alone, go, go," while Mother buffed him all over with a damp dish towel. Not satisfied, she carried him upstairs for an early bath.

Anna squeezed a sponge into the sink and said, "I guess I'll wipe up the floor." She bent down and brushed cheese and shards into a pile near my chair. "After I'd grated all that. And the bowl."

"Don't worry about the bowl."

Still squatting, she looked up. "Betsy?"

"What?"

"I can't please any of you anymore."

"You can if you try."

"Oh?" On all fours, she edged closer, open mouthed, a large depressed pet. She had no idea who she was. I could have told her anything then. ("Oh?" "Yes?" "I am?")

Through the evening she stayed tame, at the table speaking softly, after dinner gladly rinsing all those sauce-stained plates and stocking the dishwasher alone. Then, a night of broken sleep (in a sleeping bag on the living room floor—she could have joined Mother on the sofa bed, but she adamantly shook her head no), and she was Miserable Anna, snarling at her leash again.

But withdrawal is nothing new for her, and as usual, within twenty-four hours, she warmed. At the end of the week, when we hugged goodby at the airport, she said, "Betsy,

I don't want to leave you. I'll try to come back soon."
Every few days the police call for information, but what more can I say? I would quote from old letters if I could, but when one arrived, annually, my custom was to tear open the envelope, skim the note, scrawled on a card with buds blooming in the margins, and then destroy everything before the mailman reached my next door neighbor's box. Still, let's see how good my memory is: "Thanks so much for remembering my birthday." "The blouse is beautiful and fits perfectly." "I love the orchid sweater." "Candles burn in the candlesticks this second, even though it is mid-morning, sunny and bright, here." "Kiss each other for me. Love, Anna."

We "remembered" her birthday because she remembered ours, along with wedding anniversaries, and for the strange things she sent us (painted papier mâché boxes, four rag rugs the size of place mats, a string game, several unassembled kites, and books, books, and more books, probably because they can be sent fourth-class special rate), we had to repay her somehow. Actually, I enjoyed wasting time once a year, jamming plastic hangers down sportswear racks, picking through piles on display tables, occasionally asking for something out of reach that struck me as particularly hideous. It was fun to go after what I'd never want for myself (thank God), what I hoped I'd never have to see again. I bought it, asked for a box, and shipped it parcel post to insure that it would reach her days, if not weeks, after she celebrated. Of course, I spent a fair amount for these things and gave the price tags to Mother, who could be depended on to do her part unwittingly by telephone. "Anna, did you get the package from Betsy yet? Oh, I'm sure you will, any day now. I hope you like it. Don't tell her I told you, but you better like it, she spent thirty dollars for that peignoir set."

When the battered box, which had travelled by land across the continent, finally arrived on Anna's doorstep, I imagine she cut the scratchy twine with scissors she'd had handy for days, in anticipation. The brown paper, already torn, would peel off easily; the pink gift wrap, if I bothered with it that year, would be next; and then there'd be the box itself, from Teenland, Artifactory, Cuddle Up, or any of the worse stores, and dented probably. The lid would shake in her hands. She would be breathing hard enough to blow the inner tissue sheets apart. And after lifting out that cheap-looking expensive robe and nightgown, dripping lace and embroidered LONELY; after trying on the mis-sized plaid blouse (the tag said six but twelve was more accurate) with the flapped yellow breast pockets; after stepping back and realizing that the frosted glass candlesticks still looked like frozen slush, even from a distance; after sniffing and dabbing for twenty minutes before concluding that the very orchid mohair pullover on her back was making her nostrils twitch so; she would scream the way she screamed when she turned ten and hated the necklace our Aunt Ella gave her. That's right, another birthday down the drain, Anna.

Her optimism crushed again, my sister wouldn't merely give up, shelve the gift in her closet, and sit down to pen a thank you. She would ball the sweater, hurl it toward a wall, and shriek in frustration when it unfolded midway there. She would poke her fingers through the loosest neckline stitches, wind excess yarn around her pinkie, and tug until her fingertip swelled red. But no runs, no ravels; that mohair was sturdy stuff, and she wouldn't have the nerve to lift her scissors to it. She would stomp on the shirt, spit in its pockets, and then cram it into her laundry bag, to be drowned in a hot wash at the end of the work week. Not until she held it up, fresh from the dryer and still billowy, would she read the tag that said, "100% Polyester Fibers. Unshrinkable." In due time, after failing to smash them, she probably donated the candlesticks to a thrift shop. Only one year was she bold enough to send something (that peignoir set) back to me. "Lovely, but too small across the bodice, Betsy." Bodice? After I threatened Mother and Mother threatened her, she never tried that again. The past few years she must have calmed down over honey-lemon tea and iced cookies before composing the sweetest notes to us.

"Kiss each other for me. Love, Anna." Kiss each other where, Anna?

We are really alike, my sister and I. I am just waiting for her to become herself. On paper she was powdered sugar; in person, gloom, doom, and superiority. Don't you think we saw the contradictions, Annie? She struggled to keep her distance from me (after all, until she disappeared she lived thousands of miles from here), but sometimes, in adolescent desperation (though she should have outgrown *that* years ago), she telephoned. "Dates," I always summarized after she stopped crying. "Boys. Things between people never go perfectly. Why don't you get married already?"

After she's found, before long, she will marry. And after that, she will have children. She will do what I've done. Except I did it first, Anna. Remember that when you need advice about colic, drapes, finances, and the drudgery of a sixth anniversary.

Enough. I must get the salads ready. Solomon just turned into the driveway, and Stefan, smearing the window with his fingers and tongue, gurgles, "Daddy, Daddy," from the living room. I glance out the back door, and for just a moment I think I see my sister, her dark eyes peering out from inside Stefan's log cabin playhouse. I shudder, decide it's nothing, and towel the lettuce dry.

"Bitsy-Betsy," Solomon calls.

"Coming, Solo."

I move to close the door and catch her eyes again.

No, it can't be.

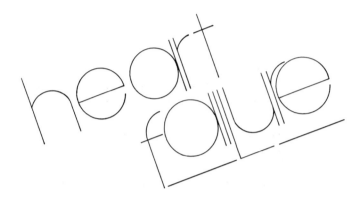

heart failure

"You'll be the death of someone," my mother said. Who? Under piled woolen blankets, I lay awake, frightened.

In the morning I saw my father, still reading at the breakfast table. "Past seven," I said. "Isn't it late for you?"

"Don't rush me."

"I didn't mean anything."

He looked up from the creased page of his paperback. "I hate my job," he said, "but I do it for you and your mother and your sister. I'm killing myself for you." He stood up and cleared his bowl and tea mug off the table. He gave them to me. "So you clean up for me. Though it won't begin to even things."

"What do you want from me?" My fingers sank into bits of oatmeal clinging to the rim of his bowl. "What do I ever ask you for?"

"Time and money. I have neither." He slipped his book into his bathrobe pocket and walked out of the kitchen.

.

"No, I can't talk to you," he said later in the entranceway. "I have only four minutes to get to the bus stop." He buttoned his topcoat over his suit. He wrapped his gray scarf over his neck and mouth and through the thick wrappings, muttered goodby to me.

.

The phone rang. "Your dad is here," Mrs. Roberts said. "At my end of the block. He's in trouble. Get your mother. Tell her I've already called an ambulance."

When I woke my mother she said, "I don't believe you," and slapped me.

"Why would I lie?"

"You would do anything to hurt me, wouldn't you?"

"He's sick. I'm going to him."

.

At the corner, Mrs. Roberts was covering him with a bright green afghan. I bent down to help. My father's long body lay solid green in the packed-down snow. His dark hair and brows shone with a dampness that felt icy against my fingertips. "Is he asleep?" I asked, but no one heard me.

The ambulance whirred as my mother ran down the street in her cloth coat and plaid pajamas. "No," she shrieked when a medic stretched the afghan over my father's face. "Why has this happened to me?"

.

At the house I watched her dress darkly without
jewelry. "You were the last to speak to him." She fastened the tiny
buttons on her blouse. "What did you say to him?"

   "Nothing."

   "Did you threaten him? Did you tell him you
wished . . . ."

   "Mother, stop!"

   "You're right," she said. "I know. So why bother
asking?"

     ·

   Out of town relatives with a poodle drove my sister
home from college. She dragged her white suitcase into the living
room, and I ran to her while the poodle barked at my stockinged
legs. "I'm going back to school next week," my sister said. "This
won't change my life. For me, this changes nothing."

   "Get that damn dog out of here," my mother said.
"Or else," she looked at me, "someone kill it for us."

     ·

   "What happened?" the relatives asked while we
ate the cold cut sandwiches they'd brought for dinner.

   "The doctor said sudden heart failure," my mother
told them. "For what that's worth."

   "You don't believe him?" an aunt asked.

   "I have information that sheds a different light on
things." My mother sipped her soda. "Yes, I think I know
something, but I'm not talking."

     ·

   I couldn't sleep that night. I wandered in the cold
upstairs hallway, hoping I would find someone there. "Daddy?"
I said when a hand grasped my arm.

   "What's wrong?" My mother laughed. "Don't tell
me you miss him. You can't hide the truth. I know."

   "What will you do to me?"

   "Nothing." She took my face in her hands, brought
it close to hers, like a mirror. "For now."

•

At the cemetery I stepped carefully over the crisp
top layer of snow. Fine cracks spread under my boot soles. Around
me, people smashed heavily through the crust to the softness
beneath, trapping themselves in their own footsteps.

"I can't go on," a cousin apologized breathlessly.
"I have my own heart condition."

My mother nodded, then squeezed my blue-gloved
hand. "Don't you turn back," she said to me. "I want you here.
Every step of the way. I want you to get the feel of this place."

She stood next to me, pressed against me, by the
grave, cut through layers of snow into the gray frozen earth. The
coffin hung suspended over it.

"Your father's in there," my mother whispered.
"Cold."

•

Afterwards people crowded the house.

"The funeral director or someone complained
because I was slightly tranquilized. Can you believe it?" My mother
shook her head. "What business was it of his? Besides, I didn't
think it showed."

"It didn't to me," a husky voice said. "Are you still
on them?"

"No, I've been realistic for hours. It's almost
unbearable."

"What about her?" A blurred man pointed to the
edge of the sofa, where I sat with a floral cushion in my arms. "Is
she drugged?"

"My younger daughter?" My mother took the
cushion from me and smoothed my hair. "No." She smiled.
"I don't think so."

•

In the kitchen she said, "You're taking this death
too hard. Visibly." She spooned through a pot of stew someone
had given us. "Do you hear me?"

"Yes."

"Who brought this stew?" she asked my sister, who was cutting into an apple pie neighbors had baked. "There's no meat in it."

"Aunt Lena," my sister said.

My mother turned to me again. "Look at this food. Pies, stew, yellow cake, brownies. From sympathizers, all of it. They want to sympathize, so let them. Talk to them. Don't hug pillows and fade into dreamland." She gripped the back of my neck with her hand. "I forbid you to."

•

A freckled woman moved close to me in the dining room. "I knew your father long ago. Tell me, were you and your sister close to him?"

"No."

"Oh, he was a very private person, Louise." My mother's voice cut in from behind. "That's what my daughter means. If we had let him, he would have spent his life in our attic with some cheap historical novels, his favorite mug, and a teapot."

The woman looked at me. "How sad."

"Well," my mother said, "not exactly."

•

I couldn't sleep again. In the dark I crept into my sister's room and switched the light on.

"What?" She sat up, her hair tangled, her lips dry.

"Talk to me about Daddy."

"What time is it?"

"Three."

"If Mother finds you in here . . . ."

"I don't care. Please, talk to me."

"He isn't worth it. No one knew him or liked him. Not even Mother."

"Then why did they marry?"

"It was a mistake." She brought the heavy bedcovers over herself. "Now get out of here."

•

"I can't wait to be back at school," my sister said. I stood with the relatives, who were leaving, too. I started crying. "Stop it," my sister said.

"Don't worry about *her.*" My mother handed my sister a folded square of money. "And don't waste this. After all, our wage earner has departed." She laughed, and the relatives joined her.

"I'm glad you're taking this lightly," one of them said. "Really, that's the only way."

An uncle picked up my sister's suitcase, and a cousin opened the front door.

"Oh, wait. Please." I ran to my sister and hugged her.

"You can't go on like this," she whispered. "I told you. He isn't worth it."

"Girls." My mother fit herself between us like a wedge. "Say goodby."

•

We were alone together. In the drafty hallway we faced each other, wearing only our nightgowns.

"You'll get up for school tomorrow."

"No."

"You're going."

"Just one more day."

"Why should I give you one?"

"Because I need one."

"All right, I'll bargain with you. For two days, maybe three. If you confess to me. Detail everything."

"I didn't do anything."

She threw her head back. "Oh, didn't you? I'll wake you for the early bus, at six thirty."

•

"I wished him dead."

She brushed her hair. "Yes?"

"I thought he might as well be dead. I thought he was already dead."

"So you killed him?"

"No."

"But you said . . . ."

"I just wished him dead."

She laid her brush, bristles down, on her glass-topped bureau and lifted the bottle next to it. "But he died," she said, shaking blue lotion from the bottle onto her hands. "You killed him."

"I didn't."

"You did. Take your mother's word for it. And turn the light off on your way out of her bedroom."

•

She was eating breakfast.

"I give in," I said. "I did it. I killed him. Will this stop now?"

"No." She poured coffee in her cup. "Life continues. Until we end it."

•

"End it," I begged in the afternoon. By the window I stood next to her, watching the snow fall.

"Do you know what you're asking for?"

"Yes."

"Then why are you crying?" She clasped my head in her hands. "Soon it will all be over."

"Good morning, yes, I'll connect you."
Each summer for four summers (with
July Fourth free, sixty-five work days
between Memorial and Labor), she had answered telephones. In
the fall, when "How did you spend your vacation?" echoed down
dormitory hallways, she rushed into the bathroom; and if cornered
near the sinks before reaching a stall, she whispered, "I answered
telephones." Amid mealtime chatter of mistaken bus rides through
the worst slums in London, the comfort of European trains (she
knew only the discomfort of the sooty commuter to Philadelphia),

unlocked hall toilets in a hostel in Spain, the blouses in Athens, the
sandals in Florence, the men all over, and the scent of one's
leotard after two months of not bathing (she had showered at seven
each morning for as long as she could remember), she prodded
her cutlet and in the distance heard ringing. But that was in
college. "On line three, it's your wife, Mr. Lawrence." And this
was forever.

Her mother in Camden said, "Now that you've
graduated, surely you could have found something better."

"No." She squeezed her receiver. "I couldn't."

From Boston, her sister called. "You're throwing
away your education." And then in a softer voice to her son on the
floor, "Please pick up your cookie."

"What?"

"You're still looking, aren't you? Every day you
should sift through the classifieds. Use part of your lunch hour."

"I don't get a full hour."

"Mother is scandalized. She doesn't answer when
people ask what you're doing."

"Who asks what I'm doing?"

"It's your life, you've chosen it. Oh, my doorbell.
Goodby. I have to get off the telephone."

It wasn't "demanding work" (her mother's phrase),
but when four rang at once, it could be confusing. "Good morning,
hold on please. Good morning, hold on please. Good morning,
hold on please. Good morning, hold on please. Yes, sorry to
keep you waiting." She never lost a call. Her supervisor said,
"I'm more than satisfied," and raised her salary fifteen cents an hour.

As a girl, she had dialed herself with three secret
digits she discovered while watching a repairman. Seven-eight-
seven, hang up, and your phone started leisurely ringing. What
urgency was there for blankness, dead current, or at most, your
older sister, who had picked up, too, on the upstairs extension.
"Hi." "Hi." "Where's Mother?" "Still in the kitchen."

But now it was different. Outside calls burst in,

the stranger the caller, the sharper the ringing. "Good afternoon, no she's not, may I take a message?"

"If you can take a message. Can you write, baby?"

"Yes, sir." She rested the phone on her shoulder and dug her fingernails into her hairline. "I'm waiting."

Ginny, who worked at the end of the corridor, laughed and advised, "Whatever they say, don't take it personally. Or it'll kill you. After work, forget work. What about tonight? Busy?"

She looked up from her desk. "I'll probably read. And talk on the telephone."

"What fun. That's against the law, you know, just dialing anybody on the telephone."

"No, I don't just dial anybody."

But when she was thirteen, at her last and only slumber party, while the hostess and the other guests shouted to passing cars from the porch, she sat at a dusty desk in a basement full of laundry and dialed every gas station in the phone book. "You made me pregnant," she said again and again to the night attendants. She cried. "What am I going to do? I'm already big, I'm so pregnant."

She had been the first of her classmates to learn about sex, but she was the last actually to understand it. In eighth grade, though, for several months, her reputation spread, and confused girls telephoned with questions. "Will I conceive, slow dancing with my father?" "No, or else he wouldn't ask you." "What about my brother's bath water?" "What about it?"

When she was eighteen a boy she never saw again entered her on her bedroom floor on a summer night, while her mother slept down the hallway. "What do we do? Push?" she asked. In the heat they lay stacked, not moving.

"No, it's over," the boy said, sliding out. "I'll try to call you tomorrow."

For two semesters in college, she had a lover. Twice a week, uneasy on his bed, they stared silently at photographs he had taped on his ceiling; but alone in their rooms on other nights, miles of campus between them, they clutched telephones and whispered for hours in the dark about their bodies. "Your breasts," he said again and again. Her ear burned from the heat of the receiver. "Yes," she said. "Tell me."

When they separated, her mother said, "But I thought you were going to get married."

"No," she said. "I wanted his voice, not his body."

"What are you talking about? What's wrong with you?"

Every night now, her mother called, still asking, "What's wrong with you?" Her sister called on Saturdays and in a crueler voice explained, "You're wasting your life, that's what's wrong with you." Her mother said, "Your sister said . . . ." Her sister said, "Mother said . . . ." They were one person with two numbers. She changed her own to "Unlisted" and escaped altogether.

From her new number, she heard only recorded voices: "The time is nine fifty-eight, exactly." "Sunrise tomorrow at six ten, high in the mid-seventies with some cloudiness late in the day, turning to showers on Wednesday." "Hello! Get ready for quick cheese balls rolled in walnuts, a lovely main snack at a party for about twenty. This is the day before, by the way, and you'll need forty-five minutes from start to cleanup." "You're a great gal. I enjoy talking to you. Really, *I like you.*" "You're a great guy. I enjoy talking to you. Really, *I like you.*" "You're fat. No, you don't want ice cream. Stay away from that plate of brownies. You're fat, fat, fat, fat. But inside you is a svelte, satisfied person." She was anyone, she was no one. Laughing, she rapped her knuckles on her hip bones.

Only in dreams was she troubled, by desperate calls cut off in the midst of her dialing (why did her fingers keep slipping?), by receivers lifted on phones that wouldn't stop ringing ("Good morning, good morning, good morning"). On the other end someone was dying; she had to get through to him. Then came the buzz of her clock, like the shock of an intercom. Awake, she finally answered herself. "Yes, good morning."

At work, all morning, "Good morning." All afternoon, "Good afternoon." And before she left at four thirty, "Have a good evening, everyone."

"I apologize for the monotony." Her supervisor smiled. "But it's over. We're promoting you now."

On the landing of the fifth floor stairwell, he helped her onto a stool in a glass-walled booth. "Our Information Center. An experiment. Just do what you can for those who call. Well, I'll be seeing you." When he shut the door, a light went on, a fan whirred, and the telephone rang.

"Information. Yes?"

"Where can I park near the Medical Center? And don't say the Walnut Garage. I won't pay those kinds of prices."

"I'm at Fiftieth and Montgomery. Where can I catch the 52W? How should I know if this is the north or southwest corner? No, toward the river, stupid."

"Help me. There's a man who wants his knife in my back."

"What size is your bra? I'm doing a little poll for Playtex, sweets. Come on, you sound bigger than that."

"Mommy, I'm hungry, where are you? Get crackers and milk. I want milk."

She did what she could ("There's street parking on Thirty-fourth, I think, if you get there early enough. . . . You should probably take the 40D, westbound, and transfer at . . . . Have you called the police? . . . I'm not your mother. Where do you live? Go to the neighbor's house. . . ."), until she couldn't anymore ("I don't know. I don't care. I don't care to know. How should I know?"). Even on the street, if people asked the time, which way downtown, she screamed at them, "Leave me alone."

But they wouldn't leave her alone. Questions dripped out when she turned on the tap. Queries blew from cupboards and drawers. "How can I?" "Where am I?" "Help me, which is it?" Even silence wasn't silent. Rooms hummed: open lines waiting for calls.

She called. "Help me, I'm pregnant. I'm hungry. I'm fat. When is the sunrise? I'm dying. I'm starving. I'm fat, fat, fat, fat. Will you help?"

"Yes. Lie back."

They dialed through her: seven jolts, a hesitation, and then the ringing.

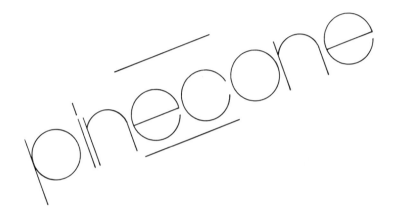

That summer at Pinecone, a sanatorium
and retreat in the Adirondacks, all the
men, homosexuals, suffered from
muscle and bone diseases, and all the women, heterosexuals,
were either over-eating or starving themselves. On June 29th,
a heterosexual male checked in.

Randolph L. (palsy, extreme anxiety) was a
twenty-eight-year-old sporting goods magnate whose specialty was
hang gliders. Throughout dinner he told sordid anecdotes, and
afterwards, in his bright narrow clothing and silver jewelry, he

sat on the terrace wall with two dozen women and swatted mosquitoes. A returning visitor to Pinecone, he discussed "the neighborhood" and recounted past stays, spent dawdling at the local garden bar, mostly. "I still have friends there. I used to date the bartender's daughter." While he spoke, Sara R. (83 lbs., 5'4") watched his single earring sway and felt very sorry for him.

When she first arrived, life at Pinecone had been difficult for Sara. Who was she? She didn't know herself; how could she tell strangers while seeding watermelon chunks? When asked her name, she managed "Sara," half of it. She had a surname, but she couldn't pronounce it. She often gritted her teeth to keep from shaking. In front of people, at group meals, she could eat only what was easily eaten. She devoured lunches, though, ripped from cardboard boxes on her bedroom floor. While everyone else digested breakfast, at nine thirty she crunched carrots and pried apart bone and chicken meat. She was famished.

People saw her hug herself, as if for warmth, on the warmest days. At the ends of meals, they saw her full plates. They saw her fingers scour her arms for a bit of flesh to clutch. They were nice to her; they felt sorry for her. Now, with Randolph, it was her turn to be nice, to feel sorry.

He wasn't spastic, but stylized. In awkward moments on the stairs, he had to coax one leg, but wasn't she herself hesitant on escalators? Limbs, instead of carrying, must be carried sometimes, or dragged, if need be. She thought she'd try to fall in love with him.

She sat near him during meals and experimentally flirted. She watched him spoon powder from a paper-bag-wrapped can and add it to his breakfast porridge. He watched her watch him. "This," he said, "looks like supplementary protein, but it's really strychnine. Want some?"

She laughed. "I don't need any. I'm killing myself by other means, remember?"

"That's not funny, Sara. What if we get together tonight? I'd like to talk to you."

"What about?"

"Whatever."

Sara spoke as little as possible about herself, but that night, alone with Randolph in his room, drinking the wine he'd stolen from Pinecone's cocktail cabinet, she relaxed. "If I want to kill myself, I should just kill myself. I can't stand eating, but eating's all I think about. . . ."

"No, don't kill yourself," he said. "How old are you?"

"Twenty, and spoiled in all the worst ways."

"Oh, Sara." When he put his arm around her, his wrist hooked. "Just nerves," he said. With his other hand, he soothed himself. "Sara." Her name again. "I want to smell you."

He was angular, she was angular, their coupling almost two-dimensional, and when certain bones rubbed, painful. But he knew what he was doing. He knew, and though she enjoyed herself, she felt as if she were a new hang glider, being test rated.

Afterwards, he whispered to her. Yes, her arms were too thin, but the rest of her, piece by piece, the rest of her.

"Don't lie, please. I'm emaciated." She rolled away from him.

"But you're one of the most passionate . . . ."

"Stop."

"Right, I'm doing all the talking. And you haven't said one thing about me."

What could she say about him, after trying not to look at him? "You're fine."

"It was as good for me as it was for you."

"It was wonderful." She waited. "Thank you."

"Did you notice my stomach?" Squeezing, he towed her fingers over rows of ridges.

"Cysts?"

"No, no. Muscles. I do exercises."

"Oh." She looked. From his middle a discrete band rose, as if under construction. She touched it again. It dimpled.

"Okay, okay, enough of that. Let's talk Pinecone. I like you, Sara."

"I like you, too."

"Yes, great, but we're not girlfriend and boyfriend," he warned. "At Pinecone, it isn't done. People play the field. For example, yours truly." He held up both his hands and using women's names instead of numbers, counted every finger. "Sara" was the tenth one. "See?"

"My God, you have a harem here." She thought of competition, of fungi spreading. She sat up. What had she done? But when he rubbed her breasts and pulled her back to him, inside she unknotted again. And she remembered why she had done what she had done. He let go. She plumped the pillow and slid her head under. Through the feathers, muffled, she heard him moving away. When she looked up next, he stood beside the bed and offered her a bundle. "What's that?"

"Your clothes. Listen, Sara, I thrash, and on a narrow mattress . . . ."

"Please, no, don't explain." She stood, sorted blouse from skirt and fussed with zippers, buttons, armholes. "Could I have some light?"

"Sorry." He flipped a switch. "Oh, look." Cellophane crackled. "Here's a present. Three rye toasts. Good for you. Eat."

Nervous, laughing, she took the package and swung it by its flap. "So we'll be friends?"

"Sara, of course."

"Let me help fix your bed." She dropped the crackers on the night stand near the "Pinecone" pamphlet and three bottles of pills. Now, to find the top sheet, she thought. She remembered they had kicked it down and crushed it with the blankets at the foot of the bed. But she only saw the bottom sheet, wildly stained, when she turned. "Oh, no, my period. Randolph, look, my period started."

"Jesus."

"Really, I'm sorry, I'll . . . ."

"Don't bother."

She touched his arm. "Will we do it again?"

"Sure. Sure we will. Here, your shoes."

She slid them on her hands. Barefoot, she tiptoed away. We'll do it again, but when? When? When? With fury, she kicked her heel sore against a banister on the way downstairs. When?

Never. He ignored her. In his gaudy clothes, he sulked when he saw her, and as if tortured, occasionally he said, "Hello." She wanted to scream, to pull taut the slack of his neck chain and tell him she had been the generous one. How could he scorn her? She should scorn him. But then she remembered: he had seen her, her breasts, swinging from her skeleton, her blood, his sheets. If only to torment herself, she had to check those sheets again.

Certain he was out (she saw his coupe round the drive), she crept up to his room and flung back the quilt. But after three days, the linen had been changed. It was a clean bed.

·

Sara: "He made me want him. He made a fool of me."

Elizabeth: "I was his first. Just two times, though. He was very good, but he wasn't very nice."

Caroline: "Sara took it hardest, I think, because she's so naïve. I heard she even bled. But the encounter was lovely and unexpected for someone my age."

Georg: "I distrusted his eyes. Considerable pouches hung beneath them. If I may speak for most of the men, we weren't at all interested. He was wan, rude, and unsightly. It only goes to show how desperate the women were."

Edwin: "I agree with Georg. We didn't need him. And he aimed for the women from day one."

Gayle: "He looked like a cabana boy, skinny, shaking, and then he made friends and came on like a gigolo.

Technically excellent. As if he'd walked out of a sex manual and into Pinecone."

Ramona: "He was too good, and he knew it. He told me himself on the terrace, 'I'm good.' So he thought he could treat us any damn way. And let's be honest, there was no market. He was our only one."

Pat: "I gave him amphetamines a few times and four or five matchbooks. He said he wanted 'to repay the favor.' I didn't realize until afterwards how methodical he was. He knocked down all twenty-four of us."

Claudia: "What he did precluded intimacy. And he created dissension among friends."

Lynn: "We all met at the pool that day to talk it over. But we didn't plan anything. What happened just happened, you know?"

•

At noon on July 7th, Randolph arrived at the Pinecone pool, approximately one-quarter mile from the institution's main buildings. He was wearing cut-off blue jeans, and he carried the regulation cardboard Pinecone lunch box. On the grass, two men lay asleep under a beach blanket. Twenty-four women sprawled on twenty-four lounge chairs surrounding the pool.

"Hi, Randy." A woman spoke. "Going for a swim?"

"No, I came to eat." He balanced his lunch box on the arm of a wrought iron settee. "Didn't bring my bathing trunks."

"What are those?"

"Shorts." He hitched his thumbs into the hip pockets and tugged. "Get these wet, it's like going in with shoes."

"So take them off."

"Yeah?"

"Sure, Randy, take them off. What do we care? We all know you, right?"

"Right." Laughing, he stripped to orange jockey briefs and draped the jeans over a rung of the ladder to the diving

board. He spread his arms and stood astride. "Do you like?"
Several women whistled. "Yes, Randy."
"Watch this." Casually, favoring his left side, he
limped toward the pool, approached the edge, and walked over it.
For a moment, caught in that big step before he touched the
water, his fingers splayed and his toes shook. Then he hit.
Twenty-four women on lounge chairs clapped. He surfaced
gasping in eight feet deep. "Hey." His one arm stretched toward
the rim of the pool, but his wrist hooked. He missed. "Hey, I have
cramps. Hey." He bubbled under. He kicked up. He thrashed.
"Hey, somebody. Cramps." He cried, but twenty-four women
didn't lift a finger. "Hey, help. My legs, help. Help! Help!"
When he floated facedown to the shallow end,
Sara slid in and waded out to him. Hair fanned his head. Sara
dipped her hands, found his chin, cupped it, and lifted; hair stuck
to her. From the mouth, from the nose, he drained water. "How
could we?" she said. "How could we?" Then she dropped him, he
smacked, and she climbed out of the water.

resignation

aybe I should look for a serious job
again, to tide me over. I think for a
minute and then howl with laughter.
What else to do at 6:00 A.M.? Too cold to type, and for the Tuttles
below me, too noisy. My fingers are numb, and the north wind,
creeping through crevices, scatters the scrawled tablet sheets I'm
transcribing, the report of some ass foolish enough to answer the
file card I tacked near the dryers in the neighborhood laundry:
"I'll type for you. Reasonable. Call Arleen, 434-7156." Yes,
I often use aliases, but exactly whom am I protecting?

I baby-sit under my real name (should I say professionally?), and the Denenbergs are expecting me at six thirty. No time left even to catnap. When page 17 of the report on local trash facilities seductively drifts my way, I only scan it and let it pass. With a free finger, I stir cream that settled (how long ago?) in some cold coffee. Not bad, if you need it. Then, spotting a long-lost acrylic scarf, I wind it about me before it gets away again: head, chin, neck, shoulders, under the arms, and knotted just below the breast line. In weather like this, I need all eighteen feet of it. Also, one has to compensate for other things: my coat, for example, which is of the blanket variety. A dime a dozen in Tijuana, so I hear, but I wasn't fortunate enough to grab it off a discount rack in the Mexican sunshine. Even now I hate to think of the small fortune I spent for it locally. I hate to think of it at all. I hate to look at it, seasonally resurrected just days ago from trunk storage in my closet. But when you're cold, you're cold.

The wind, the wind, which is even worse outside, and the rain, which I hadn't accounted for. Stoic that I am, I traipse on anyway, half a mile, to a block crammed with the most colorful townhouses. A bit like petits fours or dyed milk chocolates. I'm hungry, I guess. Food is another thing I haven't quite gotten the hang of.

As usual, Fresh (the wife, mother, scholar of the Denenberg clan), bundled in mauve crushed plush, distractedly opens the door for me. "Go up to the playroom," she says. Our eyes never meet, but somehow (through odor?) she knows me. Or maybe she's just been lucky. I could be the homeless shopping cart hag who wanders the neighborhood and is lucid enough to ring a bell this morning and nab a townhouse dog or baby. But no, I'm Amanda Arnoff, I'm safe, and though in perpetual need of cash, I'd never consider kidnapping, a federal offense, F.B.I. and all.

"Sammy's crying," Fresh says. She bends her head to one side, listens. "Or is it Elspeth? Damn." And she takes another sip from a brandy snifter half-filled with some kind of nut milk. "What exactly is in there?" I asked once on a sunnier morning. "Protein, protein, powders, and seeds," she answered. "Don't bother me."

This morning, however, while I shed water and layers, she questions me about a book that's missing. "Have you seen it? Aqua and white. Stories by Lessing."

"No."

"I don't want to accuse." She swallows. "If you walked out this morning, not only my whole day, but my whole month would be ruined. You're good with the children, or at least, you seem to be, and after Dieter and I have our monthly money talk, well, *maybe* there'll be a raise for you. So lay off our books, Amanda."

"I haven't touched your golden books." Except to read those many moving inscriptions: "To fresh Fresh, with all the love in my drum, dee dee dum, Dieter."

"I don't want to argue. I don't have the time this morning, *morning,* it's probably *noon* already."

"No, it's only . . . ."

"I know, I know." She shakes her sculpted head at my dense one. "What I mean is, if you are, I'm on to you. Stop. If you're not, my apologies."

But there isn't even time to accept her apologies. A baby wails. Again the question: who? They all sound alike, these toddlers. "The playroom," Fresh shouts. "They're both in the playroom."

And by the time I climb the stairs to them, they're both dry-eyed. "Mandy!" the one who talks (Sammy) says. For just a moment, Elspeth looks away from the white chest of drawers she's coloring. A lovely job, but I'll catch hell for it. "Mah," she says when I take her (red) crayon. But she merely makes a substitution and tenses her arm for additional embellishing in purple.

"No. No. Don't, Elsie."

And she cries, perhaps again, because it does sound familiar.

"Read to me," Sammy says. He moves closer to my elbow with his cardboard-paged picture book. "Geese."

"In a minute, Sammy. Shh, shh," I suggest to Elspeth, but she insists on crying. "Shh, and we'll all read a story."

"Morning, Amanda," Dieter (dum dee dum), attorney-at-law, calls from the hallway. "Having some trouble?"

"I'll manage it."

"Not by tolerating it, I hope."

Listen, if you're both so particular, why don't you rear your own darlings? Because you can pay fools like me to do it?

A fool, maybe, but quick with my hands. I distract Elspeth with her lobster puppet, and as she takes a breath, her shrieking ceases. Snap, snap. She sniffs and smiles.

And within the hour, quiet reigns, as Fresh, wearing green vinyl slicker over camel's hair separates, pops in "to give my loves another kiss good morning." When I first started here, she warned, "Never use the word 'goodby.' For all concerned, it's terribly disrupting." True to her theories, she sings to Elspeth about her nose and toes, runs spider fingers up Sammy's back, and she's off, for another productive day at the University.

Well gang, alone together, and now all three of us are crying. I let us moan for a while until we stop, finally. Unless there's blood, within a reasonable amount of time, there's almost always quiet. Cookies work as catalysts, but they tend to be addictive. I usually reserve the box for days when I'm overwrought and famished.

And I am very overwrought, though not particularly famished. Nevertheless, while Sammy and Elspeth indulge in morning naps, I continue my methodical exploration of this perfect household. Where did I leave off? I've already tried on most of Mrs. Denenberg's sweaters, embroidered not with the traditional red "A" but with the trademarked initials of her favorite designers. God knows I'm jealous, in more ways than one, and last week I almost walked off with a purple turtleneck. But fear overtook me, and I restrained myself. So, in good conscience,

I can sit squinting under the bright lights of any station house or courtroom and swear that I haven't lifted one Denenberg belonging. Lunch is included in this (raw) deal, and look at me, do you think I stuff myself? A strong wind could blow me over, my mother says. Occasionally, she's a staunch defender of my character.

No need to call her to the stand though, when I can use the kitchen telephone. Perched on a step stool, my coffee warm in its priceless mug ("Limited edition," Fresh lectured during my orientation period. "One of a series. They make just so many in Sweden every Christmas before the molds are smashed."), I ready myself for what could be trial by inquisitor. On the other hand, if my mother's in a pitying mood, she might send money. It's worth the risk; I can't back out now, whatever. Her phone's already ringing, and in a moment, irritated, she'll answer.

"Yes?"

"Mother?"

"Amanda? Where are you?"

"Baby-sitting."

"I knew it. At your age, still baby-sitting. If you want to baby-sit, have babies and baby-sit them. Or baby-sit your nephew and give your sister a break. Do something with your life. Your poor life."

"Mother, you know this is only temporary."

"Six months baby-sitting isn't temporary. And if I had the money to tide you over until you find a better job, I would give it to you."

"You got my letter."

"Yes, I received your threatening letter. . . ."

"It wasn't threatening."

"You couldn't find a better job if you walked into it. And I've already given you the money you asked for, when you asked for it last year. So don't ask for more, Amanda. I'll ask you, and you ask yourself while you sit all afternoon with another woman's babies, at twenty-seven, what are you waiting for?"

The diaper truck, I think, or does that stop on

Wednesdays? But who cares, and why linger on the barbs of a conversation that my mother has suddenly, mercifully, ended? I replace the silent receiver and listen to my temporary charges (yes, temporary), who are awake now and screaming. And I thank my lucky stars, Mother, that they aren't my children. I don't want children. History repeats itself, and I fear your curses would be realized. ("Your children should treat you the way you treat me, Amanda.") So that settles that. But it doesn't muffle the stretched syllables of my name, interspersed with angry shrieking. (Are you right again, Mother?) "Coming," I shout to my baby employers. "Quiet, you two, I'm coming."

They like the park best after their naps, diaper changings, and fruit juice, but today the trek is not advisable. "Don't you ever take them to the park when it's raining, don't you dare do it again," Fresh threatened months ago, after one such excursion. "I'll not only fire you, I'll . . . . Oh, I don't know what." I don't know how (well, I have my suspicions) she discovered we went in the first place. One of her friends, an adult, sits for hours on a wall there, no matter what the atmosphere. And that day someone hidden under an oilskin hooted at the children. But Fresh refused to divulge her sources. "It's none of your business how I know. A mother knows. Don't you dare question me." Maybe Sammy was already saying words by then, but I doubt it. "Go," he says now, tugging at my pants legs.

"It's raining. We can't go."

"Go." He points to the door. "Go home."

"I would love to, thanks, but certain moral and financial obligations tie me here."

Elspeth spills her milk, perhaps in appreciation, and starts clapping.

What will I do with these two? Hoping for exhaustion and a quick return to napland, I chase them around the living room, behind the down sofa and the end tables, around the wing-backed piece with the matching hassock, under the coffee table, in front of one stereo speaker and in back of the other, up to the gate which blocks the way downstairs, back to the dining room table, and on and on, until I'm breathless.

"More," says Sammy, the man of few words.

"No more," I say.

"Why?"

"Because . . . ." I hesitate and then, as usual, come up with something. "Because it's lunch time."

In the kitchen I slap together two Swiss on whole wheats, according to the rigidly adhered to Fresh menu plan, posted on the freezer. Here they are, served informally with milk (choice of bottle or glass) on high-chair trays. For some reason though, both diners open their sandwiches and laugh at the cheese slices. They peel them off the bread and carefully poke their fingers through the holes. Sammy squints through a particularly lacy section. "See?" he asks. Elspeth giggles. They both nibble a little and throw the bread to the floor. Well, more for the duck and bird bag, a bundle of stale crusts on the shelf beneath the sink, readily accessible before a jaunt to the neighborhood pond or birdbath. How organized these Denenbergs are. If I tried, I could probably learn something from them. What? I'm too foggy to think of it. Sammy rubs his eyes, Elspeth whimpers, and for the three of us, the anticipated pleasures of afternoon naptime are suddenly all-encompassing.

These two babies smell so good, I think, tucking them in after once again changing them. Well, of course they do, I tell myself, if you just changed them. These two sleeping babies overwhelm me.

And all this responsibility for so little recompense. Fresh pays me out of her spare change fund. My salary alone is a sign of how little they care for their children. And accusing me of stealing! As usual for victims of stupor, a delayed reaction. But it's never too late for revenge, and I plan mine while searching the kitchen for more coffee. I rule out murder for the sake of unknown extended family members, friends, and of course, those children. What other methods are available, and where are they hiding their coffee? Another pound is surely stashed somewhere. But I'm too exhausted to search for it, and my blur has become reassuring. More caffeine at this point would probably shatter me. And so I lie down for a while on the rag rug by the dishwasher. Thank heaven for the worn touches one can find in even the most modern household. Nevertheless, my back aches (I'm certainly losing no time in aging), and I abandon the kitchen floor for the master bedroom.

  Dieter's pornography bores me. In a bound collection of small color close-ups, a woman wearing only bikini bottoms sucks one penis after another at a pool party. Not that I have too much against orality, but I prefer to rely a little more on my imagination. Fresh does too, for in her night table drawer, I find a catalog of women's sex dreams. The titles alone are enough to do the trick for me, but not-so-distant crying interrupts the flow of things. How can you think of your own pleasure when someone tiny needs you?

  I've got to quit this job, I've got to quit this job. I sing to the rhythmic sound of a soiled diaper sloshing through toilet water. Mother, my sage, you are right. Why do I scorn you? Because, I remind myself, this bathroom is merely a way station, not a terminal. I am waiting for my ship to come in, whatever my ship is. But aren't there a multitude of way stations? I'll just find another, that's all, one a little less odoriferous. The stink I deal in here gets into your skin, under your skin, worse than onions, and you can't wash it away. Your fingers just crack from all the water. Oh, but there's one advantage: you can see your prints in scabs, the whorls in brown relief. Fingerprints, one of the few individual things about people. My marks. I leave them on the toilet seat, on the window sill (I press on both to boost myself from this unhealthy stooping-kneeling position), on the mirror, where I spread my fingers over my reflection. Great, seeing yourself fragmented in the spaces between your fingers, but not for me. I don't go in for dramatic imagery.

  Fresh, however, is a born histrionic. At a young

age, certain women are encouraged along those lines, especially if they have the faces for it. I can hear her now. "What, Amanda? You're not *really* quitting, are you? Mandy, I had no intention of offending you. The diapers? Well, just leave them if you can't stand rinsing them. I'll put a special hamper in the downstairs bathroom."

But why fantasize? Her home, her books, her diapers, her apologies, who gives a damn about them? It's her perfect purple turtleneck I'm after. I slip it on one last time while the children, flushed from their naps, play a rolling hide and seek game under the heavily quilted Denenberg bedcovers. "Now, gotcha," Sammy shouts.

"Same here," I tell the turtleneck. "And somehow, someway, we're going to leave this house together."

I retract all past words of defamation. Yes, forgive me, despite the glut of them on the market, wide-sleeved blanket coats are priceless. Wind a lamb's-wool turtleneck around your upper arm, ease into your blanket coat, and voilà, no one would suspect that you're developing right-sided biceps, concealing a thick tourniquet, or stealing. Some may wonder, however, why you're bundled in outerwear as you bask in the benefits of central heating. Let them wonder. Long ago, with foresight, you began cluttering your life with eccentricities, excuses for almost everything. Handy, yes, but they won't pay the rent, put lamb chops on the table, or make family and friends sympatico. Damn it, the old concerns have erupted again, though it's only two o'clock, early for them. And where are the children? Smothered?

No, they're sleeping again. I sit on Dieter's leather rocker and watch over them. Quiet. I try to think, until the doorbell startles me. Fresh already? Now more chimes. A bad sign, impatience. I stand up and tie my coat belt tightly in an effort to pull myself together.

But, in the doorway, all that is required of me is my signature. A uniformed man presents me with a registered parcel. "Thank you, Mrs. Denenberg," he says. I smile. I am a very friendly forger. If I'd brought my canvas shopping bag today, I could tuck away whatever it is I'm unwrapping. Dried fruit. For the sake of symmetry, I manage to stuff a package of apricots up my looser coat sleeve. There, and not that uncomfortable.

What am I doing? I stop my ascent for a brief self-interrogation on the second-floor landing. In just a few hours, I've become quite a thief. But I'm entitled to something my last day here, aren't I? No lunch. I forgot to eat any. And besides, when you work alone, you have to throw your own goodby parties.

Certainly the children won't throw one for me. The children, who are awake again. Thank goodness I'm leaving. I'm so sick of these two cranky children. "Story," Sammy demands. "Stah," Elspeth mimics. "All right, all right," I answer. I smooth out the parental bedspread and then carry both of them down the hall to their more austere playroom.

Once back among blocks and dolls, stuffed hippos and lobster puppets, they forget their need for stories. Relieved, I lean my woolen mass against the door frame. My sweat, quite profuse, will probably freeze when I hit the streets again. And where will that leave me? In a hospital with pneumonia? At least I'd get some rest then and stir up some sympathy. Oh, why am I wasting time? I should be working on my statement of resignation. Fresh, stale, where are you? I'm starting to smell like apricots, stewed in human body juices.

But wait, I hear a key in the door, the door itself swinging, and now the rat-a-tat-tat of raindrops being shaken off a green vinyl slicker. "My darlings," Fresh calls. "Mommy's home, sweethearts. Where are you?"

"In the playroom," I say as their spokeswoman. "I'd like to talk to you."

"Don't tell me you've taken them out today, Amanda."

At the top of the stairs, eagle eye that she is, she's already noticed my loot suit. But I defend myself. "No one's left

3918 Pine Street. I'm in a hurry, though, if you're wondering why my coat's on."

"Yes, Sammy, kiss Mommy," she says, puckering as he runs to her. Then to me, "Get going, if you have to."

"I want to talk to you first."

She sighs. "What is it?"

"I'm leaving."

"What are you waiting for? Is today the day we pay you?"

"Yes. I quit. Pay me."

"Well, Amanda." She smiles and strokes the heads of her children. "What do we owe you? Forty-two fifty?"

Without argument, I take it, in cash, mostly quarters, of course. It's two fifty more than Dieter would have given me.

On the street, free, but not satisfied (if I had bludgeoned her, maybe then I'd be satisfied), I unburden one coat sleeve, tear into the apricots, and with a mouthful, start running. I should have taken the prunes, too. I should have taken another turtleneck and her cabled cardigan. Regrets, regrets, and more regrets. My life story.

Other Iowa Short Fiction Award Books

1982 *Shiny Objects,* Dianne Benedict
Judge: Raymond Carver

1981 *The Phototropic Woman,* Annabel Thomas
Judge: Doris Grumbach

1980 *Impossible Appetites,* James Fetler
Judge: Francine du Plessix Gray

1979 *Fly Away Home,* Mary Hedin
Judge: John Gardner